SOMETHING NEW

FUNERALS AND WEDDINGS ~ BOOK FIVE

BERNADETTE MARIE

5 PRINCE PUBLISHING

Published by 5 PRINCE PUBLISHING & BOOKS, LLC

PO Box 865, Arvada, CO 80001

www.5PrinceBooks.com

ISBN digital: 978-1-63112-272-9

ISBN print: 978-1-63112-273-6

Cover Credit: Marianne Nowicki

To Stan,
Sometimes love shows up when you're not even looking for it. Who would have thought that a thirty second introduction would lead to thirty years? I look forward to the next thirty.

ACKNOWLEDGMENTS

To my boys, I hope I've taught you never to judge on first impressions, and that you're men enough to consider that there might be more to a person. But, I know you all very well. I think you've got that down.

To Mom and Sissy, I love our many special rituals. Tuesday, Thursday, Sunday, and all the others in between.

To Cate: Huh? What? Not quite. These are the comments that make me laugh when editing and make me a better writer when you add them. Thank you, again, for making me look good. Also, thank you for your friendship.

To my Book Hive, Thank you for your ongoing love of my storytelling.

To my Street Team and Readers, It's bittersweet to say goodbye to characters at the end of a series, but it also brings me great joy to write new ones for you. Your continued support makes me want to write for you always.

OTHER TITLES BY

THE MATCHMAKER SERIES

Matchmakers

Encore

Finding Hope

THE THREE MRS. MONROES TRILOGY

Amelia

Penelope

Vivian

THE ASPEN CREEK SERIES

First Kiss

Unexpected Admirer

On Thin Ice

Indomitable Spirit

THE DENVER BRIDE SERIES

Cart Before the Horse

Never Saw it Coming

Candy Kisses

ROMANTIC SUSPENSE

Chasing Shadows

PARANORMAL ROMANCES

The Tea Shop

The Last Goodbye

HOLIDAY FAVORITES

Corporate Christmas

Tropical Christmas

Date for Hire

SOMETHING NEW

CHAPTER 1

*M*usic echoed through the empty house. Speakers wired in every room played the same song. With one voice command, Toby Maxwell could change the song, the volume, or the location of the music. He'd had the technology long before the general public, because they'd developed the technology in his tech company, only that patent hadn't gone to them.

He had never found the need to use it to drown out the sound of the chaos in his own head before. Work had done that for him. His business had been his mistress for nearly a decade. The large house had been his trophy.

Now it all felt empty—the house and the job.

He hated when he got in his own head. But ever since his company had been infiltrated by a murderer, and his friends had been hurt, Toby couldn't help but feel that pang of guilt, and it mixed with the isolation and loneliness.

Turning on the lights in the kitchen, Toby opened the refrigerator and pulled out a bottle of water. He scanned a look over the empty shelves, which could hold platters of food. It would do him good to entertain again, but he hadn't wanted anyone in his space.

Closing the refrigerator door, Toby sat at one of the stools that circled the large island. There was no clutter on the counters like there was at Alex's house. The small kitchen in the Denver bungalow now served four, as Alex and his wife Catherine had brought home two babies in less than a year. It wasn't as quaint as Kelly and Ray's kitchen with drawings attached to the refrigerator door, drawn by their children.

Rachel and Craig's kitchen boasted a high-chair too.

The guest house a mile down the road, where Sarah and Bruce were still living, had a rustic kitchen which Toby had picked out when he'd remodeled the guest house. It, too, was quaint and cozy for a couple just starting out together.

But his own professional grade kitchen was cold and lonely, just like the house with enough rooms to house all his friends.

Before Coach Diaz died and Toby was reunited with his brothers from college, his life had been lonely. Now it was filled with those men he loved and their wives and families. But much like their lives in the dorms, when Ray roomed with Craig and Alex with Bruce, Toby had been alone.

He gave the command for the music to stop, and the silence was deafening. Pulling his phone from his pocket, he started a group text to the men who had once been known as *the fabulous five*, as Coach Diaz had designated them.

It's been a long time since we did guys' night on a Thursday. What do you say? Tomorrow night? My house? Wings and beer?

Toby sat in the silence and waited for answers.

Craig was the first. *Rachel says I'll be there.* He'd added a laughing emoji. *I miss you all.*

Bruce was the next to chime in. *Wouldn't miss it for the world.*

Ray added, *I'll be there and the kids want to come too. Anyone have a problem with that?*

They all agreed that it was fine as Alex sent his reply. *I'll bring Celia Rose. Catherine could use a break with only one baby for a night.*

And just like that, his brothers would be together again.

Feeling a little relief, Toby stood and walked out of the kitchen, leaving the light on for comfort.

As he walked through the living room, he saw a white car turn down his road, and then stop just beyond the drive.

His heart began to hammer in his chest. He could kill the next reporter to come looking for Bruce and Sarah after her kidnapping.

When the woman raised her phone to take a picture of his house, Toby headed for the front door.

~

Laura snapped her picture and looked down at her phone to see that she'd captured the essence with the sun going down behind the grand house. If only she could get an invitation inside, she could take her business to the next level. She just knew it.

"I don't know who the hell you think you are, but get the hell off my property," a man bolted from the front door and headed in her direction.

"I'm sorry," Laura stammered as she backed toward her car. "I didn't mean…"

"I don't need any reporters sticking their nose in my business."

Gripping tightly to her phone, Laura lifted her head and pushed back her shoulders. "I'm not a reporter, sir." She pulled a card from her suit jacket and handed it to him. "I'm a bridal consultant. Laura Torres," she offered as she held out her hand to shake his, but he didn't respond to that, so she pulled it back.

The man narrowed his eyes on her. "You're lost."

"No, sir. I love your house." She willed her heart to calm, and gripped her phone tighter so her hands wouldn't shake. "I think it would be an amazing venue for weddings."

"You're working with Sarah?"

Laura shook her head. "No, sir. I don't know Sarah, though if she's a bride-to-be, please give her my card."

She was sure he'd growled at her. "My house is not for rent or for show. Not now. Not ever. You can just turn back around and go."

He turned back toward the house and Laura bit down on her bottom lip.

"Again, I'm sorry, sir. Have a nice evening," she called out, but he didn't respond.

Laura watched him disappear into the house and slam the front door closed. That hadn't gone the way she'd hoped. And, if that was the owner of the house, he certainly wasn't who she thought he was. In her research, she'd found the owner of the house was one Toby Maxwell, thirty-five, and the owner of one of the biggest tech companies in Boulder. That man didn't look like the pictures of the well-educated, multi-millionaire philan-thropist. The man in the pictures was full of class and it resonated in his eyes. The man she'd met had been filled with anger and a lack of compassion. Maybe that man had been Toby Maxwell's evil twin.

CHAPTER 2

*T*here were snacks set out on the bar and the poker table. Juice boxes had been stocked in the mini-fridge for the kids, and a case of micro-brews from a new business investment were stocked in the beer cooler.

Toby had wings in the oven to keep them warm, and plenty of celery and chips to go with them.

Looking around the room, he'd overdone it. No doubt the amount of razzing he was going to take would be tremendous. But he'd missed his friends.

They'd all been through a lot in the past few months. Even he'd started seeing someone for his mental health because of it. Rachel had been right, it helped. Though deep down in his gut, he still felt guilty for what had happened to Sarah and Mindy—and Emily.

In the end, it was Toby who had hired Austin Wilkes, the man who kidnapped Sarah and Mindy and killed Emily. Toby had put him in the prime position to cause the damage he had.

Toby blew out a breath. No, he was learning to not blame himself, but it was hard. Toby hadn't hired the man. The human resource department hired him, but he'd worked his way right onto the team Toby built for Bruce. Austin Wilkes had been working a plan, and he'd played it out to his benefit. Toby and Bruce had been swindled, and a con man like Wilkes made good people think it was their fault.

Only now, Toby second guessed everything. New hires. Good employees. Old friends.

Hell, he'd nearly taken that woman's head off for stopping in front of his house. Then again, who drove down a private road and stopped in front of someone's house and took pictures? She'd had it coming, he told himself. And it didn't matter how sexy she was standing in front of her shiny car in her attractive clothes with the sun making the highlights in her hair shimmer.

"Toby?" Bruce's voice rang through the house and Toby winced because it startled him.

A few months ago having someone walk into his house wouldn't have bothered him. But things were different now.

"I'll be right up," he shouted back as he headed to the stairs and walked up to the kitchen where Bruce and Sarah stood. "Hey," he said.

"I promise she's not staying," Bruce teased as he gave his fiancée a nudge.

"It would be okay. You're one of the guys too," Toby said, hoping it sounded sincere.

Sarah moved to him, kissed him on the cheek, then opened his refrigerator and took out a bottle of water.

"The girls decided we'd do nachos and margaritas at Catherine's. Just like old times, right?"

Toby nodded. That was what he'd wanted.

Sarah opened the bottle and took a sip of water. "I'm even picking up Bruce's grandma. She wanted girls' night too. But we get brownies out of it," she teased.

Toby exchanged pained glances with Bruce. "All I have is wings."

Bruce shrugged. "We can't have everything, I guess."

They all shared a laugh and Toby thought that felt good, and he wondered if they, too, were just trying to hold it all together. After all, Bruce and Sarah had been most impacted by Austin Wilkes. Toby couldn't be the only one that felt as if he'd swallowed razors every day for months.

"Why do you have this on your refrigerator?" Sarah asked as she pulled down the card the bridal consultant had given him.

"So that I can call the police on her the next time I see her," he said with a bite.

"You're going to have Laura Torres arrested?"

"Maybe. Do you know her?"

Sarah's eyes went wide. "She's only the most sought-after bridal consultant in the area. I've called her office twice to get an appointment, and I can't get one. If you have an in, I want it."

"Are you kidding me?"

"No. Like I said, I'm having one wedding. And considering what we went through to get to this point, it's going to be huge," Sarah promised. "So how did you meet her?"

"She showed up here. I found her out front taking pictures of my house."

Bruce's brows drew together. "That's creepy."

"Right? That's why I kept her name," and her image seared in his brain, Toby thought. "If she comes back, I'm pressing charges. We've had enough excitement for one lifetime."

Sarah shook the card. "She was taking pictures of your house? Why?"

"She thinks it would be a good venue for weddings, I guess."

With the mention of that, Sarah's eyes went wide. "Oh, yes!"

"Oh, no," Toby countered. "I'm not opening my house to strangers."

"Not strangers. Us." Sarah moved to Bruce. "We should have the wedding here. It would be amazing."

Bruce wrapped an arm around Sarah's waist and pressed his head to hers. "I don't think he's open to the idea."

Sarah looked up at Toby. "For us? Seriously, it would be awesome."

Toby felt that familiar tugging in his chest, the one his therapist said was from being persuaded by others—which was something he was working on.

"Sarah, I just don't know."

She moved to him and planted a noisy kiss on his cheek. "Think about it. I would love to get married here."

How was he going to tell her no? *Was* he going to tell her no?

She held up the card. "Can I keep this? She's the best. I'd really like to try and work with her."

Toby shrugged. "I guess."

"Okay, I'm going to head out to pick up your Grandma," she directed to Bruce, "and then go to Catherine's. You boys behave."

Bruce smiled as Sarah moved to him and kissed him on the lips. "No promises," he said.

"And, Toby, those wings smell fantastic."

They watched her stroll out of the house, a bounce in her step.

Toby let out a breath and then walked to the oven to take out the wings. His head spun with everything that had just happened, and he supposed he was going to open his house to Sarah and Bruce for their wedding—and that Laura Torres woman.

CHAPTER 3

*P*inks, yellows, purples, and a shimmering blue swatch of fabric lay spread out on the worktable in front of Laura.

On each of the four walls in her design room, Laura had planning boards for the weddings she was coordinating. For some people, walking through a field of flowers or standing in the ocean would bring them a peace that lifted their spirits. For Laura, it was her design room surrounded by fabric swatches, linens, invitation samples, and seating charts. It was in the chaos of nervous brides where she shined.

The screen of her computer in the corner of the room flashed the photos she'd taken of Toby Maxwell's house outside of Boulder. Oh, he, or whomever it was that had yelled at her, had put a blemish on the house, but she wasn't done considering it for a venue.

The phone ringing pulled her from her thoughts of the house. Fridays were usually go days, and her team was out of the office finalizing last minute details for Saturday weddings. But her assistant Irene was out sick and Laura was spending Friday in the office answering the phones.

"*Laura Torres Weddings*," she said when she picked up the phone in the corner of the room. "How may I help you today?"

"Hi, my name is Sarah Burke, newly engaged," the woman said.

"Congratulations," Laura interrupted with a gleeful tone as she picked up a pen and the pad of paper that lay next to the phone.

"Thank you. I was hoping to schedule an appointment to meet with Ms. Torres to discuss my wedding."

"Well, Ms. Torres loves to discuss weddings," she informed the woman on the phone, speaking of herself in third person to give the impression that she was too important to answer her calls personally. "And whom did you say I was speaking to?"

"I'm Sarah Burke," the woman repeated. "I talk fast when I get excited."

"We're used to that. Sarah, what is your fiancé's name?"

"Bruce."

Laura wrote down the names. "And how did you come to hear of us?"

"I've had a lot of friends get married in the past few years. A few of them went through your company. I called a few times, but couldn't secure an appointment. But recently, Ms. Torres met one of my friends and left her card."

Laura tapped the pen to her cheek. She didn't like to hear that someone had told a potential client that she didn't have time to talk to them. That would need to be remedied. They didn't turn away business, sometimes they just steered it to when they had openings.

"We're grateful for your friend. Our business blossoms with referrals. Who might that have been?"

"Well not a bride. Or a groom," Sarah added. "Toby Maxwell gave me the card."

Laura's spine straightened, and not that there was anyone else in the office, but she closed the door to the design room, pulled up a chair, and sat down.

"We're grateful for Mr. Maxwell's referral. We like to send something to those who help us grow our business."

"He didn't use your company," Sarah explained. "The card was on his refrigerator, but he said I could have it."

So, she had met Toby Maxwell, and why had he kept her card? He was angry enough, he couldn't have kept it for Sarah. And then she remembered he'd asked about Sarah. It was interesting that Laura was now speaking to her. The universe had a funny way of working.

"He has a very unique home, and we live in the guest house down the road," Sarah continued, drawing Laura from her thoughts. "But I think I have him convinced to let us get married at his house."

Laura set the pen down on the table and steadied her hand on her thigh because it had begun to shake.

"You don't say?"

"Huge house, almost a mansion, and he lives alone."

A rambling bride-to-be could be filled with information. "That sounds impressive."

"It is. I'm only getting married once, and I have had to give up a few things in my life that I thought I'd always have." She heard Sarah let out a breath. That usually meant whatever they said was not open for discussion. "Anyway, I told my fiancé I was going big, elegant, and extravagant. They'll be talking about this wedding for years to come."

Laura Torres didn't know who Sarah Burke and her fiancé Bruce were, but they were quickly going to become her best friends.

"That sounds wonderful. I can arrange for Ms. Torres to meet with you and discuss dates and plans. She can meet you at your home," Laura added since Sarah said she lived on the property of the house that Toby Maxwell owned.

"Really? She'd come here?"

"Of course," Laura said, though it wasn't usually the case. "She can get a feel for the two of you together on your own turf, if you will. Most grooms are more comfortable that way."

"That makes a lot of sense. Bruce rolls his eyes when I mention things about the wedding. He's not disinterested. I think it just overwhelms him."

"Well you did say big, elegant, and extravagant."

"Exactly, and he's kind of a laid-back guy," Sarah laughed. "But he's been the only man to catch my eye since I was a little girl. It just took forever," she drew out the words, "to finally catch him and make him mine."

Now Laura pressed her hand to her chest. "Those are some of my most favorite love stories. I can't wait to get the rest of the story—I mean Laura will be anxious to hear the rest of it, and I'll hear it from her," she quickly covered her tracks. "Are you available tomorrow?"

"Wow," Sarah's voice was loud enough through the phone that Laura had to pull it from her ear. "She can meet with us on a Saturday?"

Laura winced. No, that wasn't going to work. Well, it could work. "Let me look at her schedule," she opened her phone to look at the calendar.

She had two weddings, and she didn't usually like to do that. But one was a morning wedding starting at ten o'clock, and it would be over by two. The next one wasn't until seven o'clock that evening, and on both of them she had another one of her associates taking lead. So she could easily take the middle of the day to help the dear friend of Toby Maxwell.

"Would you be available around one o'clock? She'll be between weddings, but…"

"We can wait," Sarah chuckled. "If she needs to, that is."

"Oh, she'll be happy to meet with you. Trust me." Laura picked up the pen again. "Why don't you give me your phone number and then your address. She'll meet you at your house at one o'clock."

CHAPTER 4

*A*rmed with her portfolio, dressed in her suit, which she wore to morning weddings, Laura Torres turned off the highway and onto the private road, which was clearly marked.

But this time she'd been invited.

She caught a glimpse of herself in the rearview mirror smiling. Oh, Toby Maxwell couldn't keep her away, she thought. There would be a wedding in that house, and she would organize it. He would see how spectacular it could be, and a man who lived alone in a house that ostentatious probably thought in dollar signs. A house like that had a lot of wasted space, and dollar signs were good conversation starters.

With the navigation assistant giving her directions from her phone, she slowed as she passed the big house. The grounds were still green, which contrasted with the brown earth that led to the majestic hills and mountains behind the house. There were blooming pots of flowers at the entry way. Laura's flowers never lasted past the dry July heat. So she envied anyone who could keep beauty alive like that.

Of course, he probably paid someone to do that for him.

The voice of the navigation assistant told her to continue down the road for one point two miles. As the majestic house faded in her rearview mirror, she looked ahead and admired the beauty in front of her. The line of trees on the horizon set the base for the Flatirons behind them. The range of mountains was the backdrop for the foothills of the Rocky Mountains, and the spectacular sight never grew old or dull. The house was amazing, but a spring wedding venue in the fields when they were green, with the backdrop of the mountains behind them—oh, the possibilities were endless.

As she crested a small hill, the house where Sarah and her fiancé Bruce lived came into view. Perhaps it was the original home on the land. Or a guest house, Laura couldn't be sure.

But for as big and majestic as the other house was, this one was small and quaint. For a moment, she gave some thought to the two houses and she continued to drive.

The big house would be great to entertain and show off, but a home would be warm and cozy—like the little house she was driving up to.

Laura parked her car next to the two other cars in front of the house. Before she could gather her purse and her portfolio, the front door opened and a woman stepped out onto the front porch and waved.

Setting her professional smile in place, Laura climbed from the car, shut the door, and walked toward the woman.

"Sarah, I presume?" she asked, and the woman nodded.

"That's me."

Laura walked toward her, noting that she looked very familiar, but wasn't sure she could place her.

"It's nice to meet you," Laura said as she balanced her book in one arm and extended her hand to shake Sarah's.

"Likewise. I can't believe you could meet me today. I told the woman who answered your phone that I'd called a few times and was told you were booked. So this is wonderful."

Laura continued to nod, and she swore she'd find out who told her they were too busy to plan her wedding.

"You have an amazing view," Laura gestured toward the mountains with a nod of her head.

"I'll miss this the most," Sarah said.

"Are you not staying here?"

"It's a long story. We've been here longer than we meant to with Toby's generosity—he owns the house. But, we're having a house built in Golden and it'll be done soon."

"The views from Golden are equally as nice," Laura confirmed.

"Come on in. Bruce is taking a call in the bedroom. I have iced tea and a pitcher of water on the back porch."

Laura stepped onto the porch and followed Sarah through the cute house and out the back door. She took the seat that was offered and set her portfolio on the table.

A moment later a man walked out onto the porch and Laura stood to greet him.

"Laura," Sarah began, "this is my fiancé, Bruce Griffin."

Laura held out her hand to shake Bruce's, and she realized he, too, seemed very familiar.

"It's nice to meet you, Bruce. Congratulations on your engagement," she said as he wrapped his arm around Sarah's shoulders.

"Thanks. I have to pinch myself once in a while to make sure this is real. It took us much too long to decide this was what we wanted."

Laura thought of her conversation with Sarah on the phone the day before. "You've known one another a long time, then?"

They both nodded. "I was five when I met him," Sarah said. "He's my brother's best friend."

Laura could have predicted that. Couples who had known

one another that long and took equally as long to get together usually had the obstacle of a sister or brother whose best friend fell in love with their sibling. Sometimes it tore a family apart. Sometimes it only made it better.

"I love that kind of romance," Laura noted. "Why don't we all sit and I can show you the kind of work I do and you can tell me what kind of wedding you're thinking of having."

She saw the hesitation on Bruce's face, and it was perfectly normal. Sarah on the other hand wore an enormous smile.

Laura lifted her large notebook which housed photos of past weddings, beautiful venues, gorgeous dresses, and elegant catering. It showcased all of the elements to prepare a bride and groom for that big, elegant, and extravagant wedding—like the one Sarah described when she'd called the day before.

CHAPTER 5

*T*oby finished his workout in his home gym and wiped his face with the towel. He and Bruce had a good fitness regimen going with their workouts they did at the office, in the gym Toby had put in there. But when he had nothing to do, Toby found that working out kept his mind calm. Otherwise, his brain went into overactive mode.

His company was one of the biggest tech businesses in Boulder, and getting bigger. He'd invested in a winery, a brewery, an athletic fashion line, a storage unit company, and a hydroponic farm. There was a lot for Toby to think about.

But he wasn't all business. Toby mowed his own lawn and tended to the few flowerpots. On Sundays he played basketball with his friends. They promised they'd continue to meet on Thursdays for guys' night. At least once a week he had an invitation to dinner at one of their houses.

He'd begun to think of himself as the spinster aunt that everyone felt sorry for.

Toby pulled open the refrigerator in his kitchen and took out a sports drink. His heart still raced from the cardio he'd mixed with his weighted reps.

Shutting the refrigerator door, he opened his drink and took a sip. Setting the drink on the island, he leaned in on his forearms, and scrolled through his phone. When he heard the sound of cars driving by the house, he walked toward the front door. Sarah pulled up in front of the house and parked in the private circle drive. Behind her car was the white Audi he'd seen in front of his house days before.

What in the hell was she doing back there, he wondered as the woman stepped out of her car in her suit, her highlighted hair pulled up into an elegant bun. Large, dark sunglasses shielded her eyes.

He was ready to call the police when he remembered that Sarah had taken the woman's business card off of his refrigerator. Wincing, Toby opened the front door.

Sarah climbed from her car, and Bruce emerged from the passenger side with a sheepish grin.

Lifting her glasses atop her head, Sarah hurried to him and placed her hands on his arms and looked him right in the eye. "Don't be mad, just hear me out."

He realized he had his eyes narrowed and was gritting his teeth.

"I got a meeting with her and she came to the house to meet with us. Oh, God, she's got the best designs and everything."

"Sounds lovely," Toby growled. "So why are you here?"

Sarah batted her eyes. "Consider it, please? I want to have my wedding here. It would mean the world to me."

Toby moved his gaze from Sarah to the woman in the suit, who had slid off her large dark glasses and now stood next to Bruce, smiling, her notebook in hand.

"Why my house?" he whispered as he shifted his attention back to Sarah.

"Because you were our first ally, your house is freaking amazing, and it's the most intimate and elegant setting I could ever pick."

Toby wanted to say no. Everything inside of him hated the idea of having people in his home. But he looked at Sarah who stood in front of him with those dark eyes staring at him. There was a tiny scar above her eyebrow, but it was just enough to be a constant reminder that someone had tried to kill her.

With all that she'd been through, how could he possibly tell her no?

Still feeling some of the guilt that Austin Wilkes was able to get to her, and had killed her best friend and threatened her, he felt as if he owed her. But his house...

"Well?" Sarah pleaded.

Toby let out a slow breath. "Okay."

Sarah's eyes lit up, and she pulled him in and kissed him on the cheek. "I love you. Thank you."

He wasn't sure what else to say.

Laura watched the exchange at the front door, and pursed her lips to keep from smiling too wide. He'd obviously given Sarah the okay to use the house, and Laura was about to get her first peek inside.

As Sarah waved them in, Laura walked next to Bruce and leaned in. "Is he scary? Last time I spoke to him he was scary."

"When he kicked you out?"

She winced. She shouldn't have been surprised they'd all put two and two together. "Yes."

"He's actually a pussycat. But the only things he prizes, beyond friends and family, is this house and his car."

"It's going to be a beautiful venue," she promised.

"You haven't even seen the inside yet."

Toby stepped back as Sarah moved past him into the house. Bruce fell back so that Laura could enter.

As she crossed the threshold, she looked up at Toby with dark eyes. "Thank you." Her perfume surrounded him, and there was nothing he could think to say.

Bruce walked through the door and slapped Toby's shoulder. "She's stupid giddy," Bruce said as Sarah began to lead Laura through the house.

"Which one?"

Bruce laughed. "I meant Sarah, but I guess it goes both ways. Are you sure you're okay with this?"

Toby wanted to tell him the truth, but he just didn't have the heart. "She deserves it. And it's one day, right?"

"I think so," Bruce laughed. "I don't want to seem as if I don't care about the plans, but I have no idea what I've been looking at for the past two hours. Pieces of fabric. Napkins. Flowers."

"She really wants an all frills wedding? I can't say I would have ever seen that coming."

Bruce's eyes lost their humor. "Like you said, she deserves it. She'll never have my children, and this seems to be what will make that sacrifice right in her mind."

Toby closed the front door and rested his hand on Bruce's shoulder. "Then we give her what she wants."

"Right."

"And you're probably off the hook for decisions once she gets Rachel, Catherine, and Kelly involved."

"Don't forget my grandmother," Bruce reminded him. "She seems to have a lot of opinions too."

CHAPTER 6

*S*arah had been very thorough with her tour of the house. Laura's heart still raced in her chest. She was standing in the house that had been in her sights for the past few years.

The plans and thoughts that spun in Laura's head had her nearly dizzy. The ability to set up the caterers, the number of people that could attend, the setup for the nuptials—it all swirled in her head and she couldn't wait to print her pictures and make the design wall for this wedding.

She had left Sarah and Bruce in the kitchen to discuss a few items that she'd like them to consider before they committed to working with her. Taking the stairs down to the lower level, Laura thought she'd look around the game room area again.

It could be cordoned off to keep guests on the main level. But it could also offer a great opportunity for entertainment if Toby was willing to let them use the area. Really, the possibilities were endless. The upstairs rooms could be used for the bride's suite and the game room with the spare bedroom, theater, and bar would be a groom's haven.

"Will it work?"

Laura spun when she heard the voice behind her.

Toby stood behind the bar with a glass bottle of soda in his hands.

Laura smiled and walked toward him. "It most certainly will. It's going to be a magnificent place to have a wedding, if they decide to sign with me."

Toby nodded. "Drink?"

"Do you have a bottle of water?"

He turned to the small refrigerator behind him and retrieved a bottle of water. Wrapping a bar napkin around it, he slid it toward her.

"Thank you," Laura said as she twisted off the top and took a small sip. "I would like to apologize again for the other day. I didn't mean to upset you when I came out this way. I should have respected your privacy."

Toby chewed his bottom lip as he studied her. "I'm sorry I was such an ass about it. I've driven up on properties I was interested in acquiring before, too—and was met with the same chaos I shelled out on you."

"You own more houses?"

Sipping from his bottle, Toby shook his head. "Just the one Sarah and Bruce live in right now."

"It's a nice little house."

"It is. It'll be empty soon. Their house is almost done being built," he informed her, and then shifted his eyes as if he hadn't meant to give her that much information. "Do you play pool?"

Laura turned to look at the table behind her. "You want to play?"

"I just thought since they're..."

"Yes, I play," Laura slipped her phone into the pocket of her suit coat. "Rack 'em up."

. . .

35

Toby moved from behind the bar and walked to the pool table, collecting the ball rack from the wall. He watched as Laura unbuttoned her suit jacket and slipped it off, carefully hanging it over the back of one of the high back bar stools.

Beneath the suit jacket she wore a sleeveless dress, which showed off a set of beautifully sculpted arms. Laura adjusted the pearls on her slender neck, and touched each of her earrings as if she were checking that they were both still there.

When she looked in Toby's direction, and he realized he'd been staring, his mouth went dry.

He gathered the balls and organized them in the rack as Laura inspected the pool cues, pulling one from the stand and chalking the tip.

"You can break," Toby said as he pulled the rack from the balls.

Laura lined up her shot at the end of the table, pulled back the cue, and hit the cue ball, sending it into the others.

Toby watched as the balls scattered toward the pockets, and three of them sank.

She grinned when he looked at her. "Solids," she called her next shot, and sank two more balls before it was his turn.

"I guess you do play, huh?"

Laura laughed as she balanced herself with the stick like some female warrior wielding her staff. "My grandfather ran a bowling alley. I can bowl a two-hundred-forty. I've never lost at air hockey, and I still hold the high score on the Batman pinball game. I used to hang out there after school until my parents were done working."

Toby scratched the cue ball and Laura's smile grew wider. "I guess it's your turn," he said, stepping away from the table.

Laura walked around the table and studied the balls. "What about you?"

"No," Toby cleared his throat as he admired her leaning over and lining up her shot. "My grandfather didn't run a bowling alley."

She laughed easily, he thought. Was that part of her sales tactic, or was she just easy to converse with, he wondered.

"Did you grow up around here?" she asked.

"Texas."

"I wouldn't peg you as a cowboy."

"Much like being from Colorado, not all Texans are cowboys."

Laura nodded as she moved to her next shot. "*Touché*," she said as she sunk another ball. "I've never been on a horse."

"Okay, I'm more of a cowboy than you are then," he laughed and felt the tension from being around the woman ease a bit. "I came to Colorado to go to college and that's how I met Bruce."

"I started in Santa Fe," she admitted as she watched her ball fall into the pocket. "But I was only three when I moved here. Semi-Colorado native?"

"I'd say it counts."

Her lips puckered and her eyes sparkled, and for a moment, Toby forgot that he didn't like the woman because he didn't want people in his house.

As she lined up her last shot, and she cleared the table, Sarah and Bruce walked down the steps.

Laura put her cue back in the rack, picked up her suit jacket, and pulled it back on. Toby leaned up against the pool table and watched her transform back into the wedding planner, from the bowling alley rat she'd admitted to being.

Sarah moved in close to Bruce, her hand on his chest, and his arm around her waist. "Okay, we're ready to sign contracts with you and pick a date. We love what you have to offer and I think— we think—you'll give us the wedding of our dreams."

Toby bit down on the inside of his cheek to avoid grinning at his friend's expression. Maybe it would be worth letting Bruce and Sarah use his house just to see Bruce squirm while making wedding decisions.

CHAPTER 7

*L*aura set her portfolio on the passenger seat and pressed her lips together as she started her car and pulled away from Toby Maxwell's beautiful house. When she got to the end of the road, she put her car in park and let out an excited scream that rattled the windows.

The contract to plan Sarah and Bruce's wedding was signed and they'd settled on a date.

The wedding of Laura's dreams—due to the venue—would be held around Christmas in the beautiful Maxwell home.

Laura drummed her hands against the steering wheel and let out another squeal. She couldn't wait to show Toby how she could transform the house and the grounds into the perfect venue. What good was a house that big, and beautiful, for one man? It had such potential.

Pulling off the private road and out onto the highway, Laura headed toward the next wedding venue when her phone rang. Pressing the button on her steering wheel, she answered the call.

"Laura, it's Amy. The MOB took something to sleep last night, and she's completely hungover. We can't keep her awake to get her hair done."

"I'll stop and get her an espresso. Before they do her makeup, use a cold cloth on her face."

"We need more dress tape. The bride lost another six pounds and the bust of the dress…"

"I have the emergency case in the back of my car. I'm on my way. I'll be there in twenty."

"Laura, did you get it?" Amy asked and Laura felt the grin that still tugged at her cheeks widen.

"I got it. The wedding and the house."

"Wow. Just wow. And what's the millionaire like?"

Laura thought about her first impressions of Toby Maxwell, and his evil twin persona. But she wasn't sure that was the real him. After their pool game, she was quite sure there was more to the Texan transplant.

She supposed if she was going to work her way into using his house for more than one wedding, she was going to have to get to know the man who hid in that enormous house alone.

"I think he's a lonely millionaire who just wanders through that house."

Amy let out a hum. "Sad-looking?"

"No," Laura realized she'd answered very quickly.

She thought about how Toby had looked when they'd arrived at his house. He'd obviously been working out, by the gym shorts and tank top he'd worn. His dark hair had been damp, and there was a pink glow to his skin that said he'd had his blood pumping.

Toby Maxwell was tall, basketball player tall, she thought. With dark eyes that questioned everything, and a well-groomed beard that accentuated kissable lips.

Laura cleared her throat and shook the thought from her head. "He's handsome."

"You sound flustered. He must be sexy as hell."

Laura gripped the steering wheel tighter. "He's handsome," she reiterated, keeping her voice calm.

"Can't wait to meet him," Amy said. "Get that espresso here. She's snoring in the chair."

"On my way."

～

Toby tied his high tops and watched as his friends and their families walked into the gym at the YMCA. Sunday mornings had been set aside for basketball games with his college brothers since their coach had passed away and they'd all come together to celebrate the man.

Toby hated that it took Coach's death to bring them together, and deliver an end to Toby's complete loneliness.

Ray sat down next to him and pulled his shoes from the gym bag he carried in. Ray's wife Kelly sat on the bleachers behind them and set their children up with breakfast they had picked up on their way in.

"What's new, friend?" Ray nudged Toby.

"Same shit, different day," he replied, but felt as if it sounded negative. "Took another twenty seconds off my mile," he boasted, and Ray laughed.

"Well, that's something."

Craig and Rachel were next to walk into the gym with their daughter Angela on Rachel's hip. Alex walked in alone, followed by Sarah and Bruce.

When Alex plopped down on the other side of Toby, he yawned.

Both Toby and Ray watched him, humored.

"Long night, dear?" Toby teased.

"Both girls have colds. Gretchen has a harder time nursing because of it, and now Catherine is engorged, miserable, and tired."

Toby winced at all that information. "Why are you here then?"

"She kicked me out because I was hovering, unable to help."

Resting his hand on his friend's shoulder, Toby grinned. "We won't tell her if you decide to lay on the bench and take a nap."

"I might just take you up on that," Alex yawned again.

Toby stood, walked across the court, took a ball from the rack, and turned right into Sarah's embrace. He laughed, not expecting her to have wrapped her arms around him.

"Bruce is going to get jealous," he teased.

"I'm just so happy."

"I'm glad," he said as he stepped back and admired her wide smile.

"It's because of you. I still can't thank you enough for letting us use your house."

Rachel walked past them and stopped. "You're getting married at Toby's house?"

Sarah nodded enthusiastically. "Laura Torres met with us yesterday."

"I thought you couldn't get an appointment."

Sarah rested her head on Toby's shoulder. "I mentioned that I got her card from Toby and I got an appointment right away."

Rachel narrowed her eyes at Toby. "You know Laura Torres?"

He chewed the inside of his cheek. "I do now. Let's leave it at that," he said as Craig took the ball from his hands.

"Are we playing or are you going to let the women paw all over you?" Craig teased, but Toby was grateful for the distraction to get away from the conversation about Laura Torres.

CHAPTER 8

The pictures of the house, which Laura took on Saturday, scrolled on her computer and she sat with her cup of coffee and watched them. She was sure she could drive to Vail and find a similar home on the side of the mountain, but this glorious piece of architecture was only a few miles away. The scenery wasn't any less spectacular than something that would be found on Vail mountain. The majestic Rocky Mountains and the Flatirons surrounded the property, and it was glorious.

The rustic feel, with the wooden pillars and large windows, screamed Colorado. The landscape, though well-groomed, and obviously professionally done, melded with the natural grasses in a way that an onlooker wouldn't notice the lush green ended, yet would appreciate the elegance.

She wanted pictures at sunset, with the sun going down behind the mountains in hues of red and orange. And then, she'd like another photo with the house lit up from the inside. It would be a warm picture, she thought.

The possibilities of what they could do with that house were endless. Weddings. Retreats. Receptions.

The pictures scrolled to the ones she had taken the day Toby

Maxwell threatened to have her arrested. One of the pictures was of him coming at her.

It was no wonder she considered that he'd been an evil twin. There was madness in his eyes. She supposed she deserved that. It wasn't the first time she'd been accused of trespassing on land when she thought it was just too elegant a setting to pass up looking at.

But the man in the photo didn't match the man she'd played pool with. That man was just a quiet genius, that she knew. He loved his home, didn't care much for Sarah's plans, but adored his friends enough to let them have their wedding there.

Laura leaned back in her chair. She didn't have many friends like that. None that would ask anything of her, and vice versa. Lifting her head, she looked out into the office through the glass walls of her private office. The building had once been a historically registered home, and had been gutted by a fire. When she'd purchased it, she'd had it renovated on the inside to be a modern office space, but the exterior still held that century-old charm.

Her business was her lover and her friend. The only bridal showers and teas she attended were the ones she planned for clients. Laura picked up her engraved gold pen and tapped it to the notepad on her desk. When was the last time she'd done anything outside of work? Her weekends were filled with weddings. Her weeknights with paperwork, and her weekdays with wedding planning—and not her own wedding.

The thought choked her. Picking up her coffee mug, with her company logo on it, she sipped her now cold coffee. Laura needed a life. Wasn't that why she had a staff of ten buzzing around the office at any given time, and even more on the weekends making the magic of a wedding happen? Weren't they there to help her run her business so she could enjoy what it had offered her?

She felt the flush of heat in her chest and it moved up into her cheeks. When Irene tapped on the glass door and pushed it in, Laura jumped and her coffee splashed onto her white suit.

"Shit! Shit!" She jumped up and Irene's eyes went wide.

"Shit!" she yelled too. "Are you okay? Did it burn you?"

Irene dropped the stack of items she'd carried in onto the chair in front of Laura's desk and hurried to the private bathroom to grab paper towels.

"I'm fine," Laura said as she snatched the paper towel and blotted her suit.

There was a protocol for such things in their office, because in their business, when an accident happened, it was usually on white fabric.

As Laura dabbed the paper towel over her suit, Irene pulled another suit from the armoire.

"Get changed," she instructed. "I'll get this downstairs and will start to get it cleaned."

Laura stood and took the suit. Irene's calm head usually kept Laura calm too. This was no different. Laura could lose her cool or she could quickly change, hand off the dirty suit and get on with her day.

As Laura walked into the bathroom and closed the door, she realized that the reason she'd spilled her coffee in the first place was because she'd been thinking about other things—mostly Toby Maxwell's house—and who was she kidding, she'd been thinking about Toby Maxwell too. When she peeled off her suit, she looked in the mirror. There she stood in the secrets that Victoria kept. Pathetic. What good was the secret under her clothes if she didn't let others see it?

There wasn't time for pity parties. Laura took the dry cleaning bag off of the other suit and changed.

When she walked out of the bathroom, Irene held her arms out for the soiled suit.

"The new line of linen colors just came in. They're on your desk along with the processed contracts for the Griffin/Burke wedding. Accounting says you didn't get a down payment and your lawyer says if you're using a private house that big, that doesn't belong to the party getting married, he wants an insurance policy or the owner to write off liability."

Well, obviously her mind had been in the clouds on Saturday knowing she was going to go through the beautiful house. Laura knew she needed all of those things, and usually she didn't miss a step.

"I'll get that taken care of," she promised. "And, Irene, thanks for taking care of the suit."

Irene nodded with a smile. "You looked like you were a million miles away when I walked in. You're feeling okay?"

Laura nodded. "Just had a lot on my mind."

CHAPTER 9

Toby wiped his brow with the hem of his T-shirt. He hadn't mowed the lawn over the weekend, so here he was, after a full day of meetings, sweating in the August evening.

Usually he liked to follow a schedule. There was basketball on Sunday mornings. A set calendar through the week with his work. Meetings were scheduled on Mondays and Wednesdays. Field work on Tuesdays. He didn't move from behind his desk on Thursdays, until he left early for guys' night. And Fridays were casual and made for tying up loose ends from the week.

Saturday morning was for mowing the lawn and taking it slow—but it hadn't happened that way this week.

Toby had one more pass through the front lawn and he'd be done. He'd been razzed more than once about mowing his own lawn, but why shouldn't he? Homeowners mowed their own lawns, and he was no different.

Just as he lowered to pull the cord and start the mower, he noticed a car in the distance on the road that would pass by his house.

Since Sarah had been abducted, every car that passed down the road in front of Toby's house was suspicious. Though the road only went to his house and then to the guest house, it should have always been suspicious. He'd once been comfortable knowing most cars that ended up on the road had taken a wrong turn—but not anymore.

As the car came closer, he realized it was driving to his house, and then he recognized it.

His mouth went dry as a bead of sweat rolled off his brow and into his eye. Wincing from the sting, he lifted his shirt again to wipe at his face just as Laura Torres pulled up in his driveway.

Letting out a slow and steady breath, Laura put her car in park and admired the scene in front of her. Toby had lifted his shirt to wipe his face, and hadn't that given her quite an image?

She'd seen his physique, having shown up with Sarah after he'd worked out over the weekend, but there was something raw in seeing him shine outdoors from mowing the lawn.

She swallowed hard, remembered why she was there, and collected herself. Picking up the folder from the passenger seat, Laura opened the door and stepped out of the air-conditioned car.

"Awfully hot out here," she said, smiling.

Noticing that Toby took a long scan over her, she realized she hadn't put her suit jacket on, and the fabric of the white cami she wore was very thin. Those secrets of Victoria, which she'd chosen for her other suit, were bright and bold under the thin fabric of the suit she'd put on after she'd spilled on the other.

"It is."

He was a man of few words, she thought. Or, she'd stunned him silent with her sexy bra showing through her top. Well, she wasn't going to turn around and put on her jacket. She'd melt too. Perhaps she'd let Victoria do her talking for her.

The thought warranted a giggle that bubbled in her chest, but Laura stifled it before it escaped.

Toby picked up a sports drink from the step on the front porch and took a long drink while she stood there watching. Suddenly she found she had few words too. She needed to get her head back in the game.

"I'm sorry to drop by unannounced. I have some papers that I need you to sign."

Toby lowered the drink and recapped it as he continued to study her. "Why do I have to sign anything? I didn't hire you."

Laura smiled. "Your graciousness to let Sarah and Bruce use your home requires me to have you sign a waiver allowing us to use the location."

Toby nodded slowly. "A waiver?"

"You know, not holding us liable."

"And if I don't sign it?"

"Then you have to sign another that gives us permission to be here and we'd take out an insurance policy specific to the event and your home."

Laura watched as Toby chewed his bottom lip. "These are my friends. Why would I need a waiver for my friends?" he asked as he began to walk toward her.

There was an odd fluttering in her chest, and Laura fought it off. "It's business. You understand business," she suggested.

Toby nodded slowly. "I don't just sign things. I read them."

"Of course," Laura said holding out the folder.

He didn't take it right away, instead, he kept his eyes even with hers. "Why don't you bring it inside. Let's go cool down, have a drink, and I'll look it over."

"Oh—okay," Laura's words stuck in her throat.

Pulling the folder to her chest, she followed Toby into the garage. Unable to help herself, she looked around. There were two cars parked in the garage, and one was a convertible. Wouldn't that be nice, she thought?

Toby pushed open the door to the house, and they walked into a mudroom that led to the massive kitchen.

There wasn't any part of that house that didn't amaze her, she thought.

Toby pulled open the refrigerator door. "I have soda, water, flavored water, and beer." He turned toward her. "I have also have a very nice selection of wine and tequila downstairs. I have interest in a winery in Palisade and a tequila company," he added as if he needed to say it, but the flash in his eyes told her he hadn't said it to impress her.

Laura wondered if he'd be more comfortable downstairs at the bar where they'd shared their game of pool. There had been a peace between them in that space. And, she could use a drink after seeing him all glistening again.

"I would love a glass of wine."

Toby closed the refrigerator door and started for the stairs, and again Laura followed.

"Did you design the house?" she asked as they descended the stairs.

"Yes."

"You have an amazing eye."

"Thank you."

"I was thinking, this house reminds me of those in Vail that you see as you drive through the valley. The exquisite use of logs that make it seem rustic, but everything else is modern. The ones where the sun glistens off the window," she sighed when she said it, then composed herself. "I'd love to see one of those houses too."

Toby walked behind the bar and pulled a bottle of wine from the small refrigerator. Setting it on the bar, he picked up the corkscrew and began to open it.

"You're all about location, huh?"

Laura sat on one of the stools at the bar and set the folder down. "I guess when it's your business, you can't help it. Right?"

Toby pulled the cork from the bottle and studied her. "Right."

CHAPTER 10

*T*oby pulled down two wine glasses and filled them. He pushed one toward Laura and picked up the other.

Laura picked up her glass, sniffed it, and swirled it in the glass before sniffing it again. "Nice."

Toby watched as she lifted the glass to her pink lips and sipped. She took a moment before she swallowed, and he knew she knew her wine. The woman obviously understood fine things.

"You own this winery?" she asked.

"I'm invested in it."

"The quality is consistent?"

"I made sure of that before I bought in."

She swirled the wine in her glass again. "I'm always on the lookout for nice wines for our weddings. I might have to look into them." She sipped again. "Yeah, this is nice."

Her long eyelashes batted, and Toby's breath was caught in his chest. She was breathtaking, he thought as she sat at his bar sipping wine. He didn't want to think that, but he couldn't help it.

Laura Torres knew wine. She knew architecture. She knew how to dress so that a man went speechless.

Her hair was pulled into a bun, low at the base of her neck, much as it had been on Saturday when she'd come out to the house between weddings. The hairstyle accentuated her slender neck, and made him want to trace his fingers over her collar bone, and place kisses...

That breath that had been stuck in his lungs whooshed out and he nearly choked on it. Quickly, he took a large sip of the wine to calm himself.

"I could introduce you to the owners of the winery," he found himself offering, and took another large sip.

As Laura lowered her glass, those soft pink lips turned up into a smile. "Would you?"

Toby nodded. "If you're pressed for time we could fly up there. Or we could take a drive. I mean when you're free. I know you're busy with weddings all the time. Or, when they're down here again, I could..."

"A drive sounds nice," she cut him off, and he couldn't have been more grateful.

"A drive does sound nice." Toby finished the wine and it went right to his head. "When?"

Now she bit down on her bottom lip and Toby gripped the edge of the bar. "My team is fantastic. I can tell them to take care of things any day of the week."

They had that in common, didn't they? But like him, he wondered how often she utilized that team to take time for herself.

Suddenly he wanted to jump in his car and take off, but that wasn't going to work.

"Wednesday?" he asked, realizing he'd have six meetings to move, but his brain couldn't focus on anything but those pink lips.

Laura's eyes rolled upward as if she were recalling her schedule. He knew he did that too when someone asked him to recall something.

A moment later she picked up her wine and held the glass to her mouth. "Wednesday would be perfect," she said before she sipped.

Toby refilled his glass. "Wednesday it is."

Toby finished his second glass of wine and Laura finished her first. When she set the glass down, she looked at the folder that sat on the bar between them.

She'd been there much longer than she figured he would have allowed her to be. To stay in his good graces, she should get him to sign off on the house and go collect her deposit from Sarah, but she really wanted another glass of wine.

Toby must have read her mind, because he filled her glass.

"It's right about dinner time," he said. "I have a steak marinating in the refrigerator. Why don't I cook it up, add a salad, and I'm sure I can find a bag of frozen vegetables to add to it."

Laura picked up her glass and sipped. He was asking her to stay. There was no reason she should, except to plant the seed that his house could make them both a lot of money. Staying would be mixing business with a great deal of pleasure, but she couldn't help but nod. She wanted to stay.

"That sounds nice."

"Did you need to go to Sarah's, too?" he asked looking down at the folder.

"I need to get the deposit. It appears I forgot a few steps when I was out here on Saturday."

"Why don't I get a quick shower and I'll go over with you. You can get your deposit and then we'll come back and eat."

Laura's lip trembled, so she took a sip of wine to hide it. "Okay," she finally managed, which then warranted a wink from Toby.

He put his glass in the bar sink and quickly disappeared up the stairs. Laura spun the stool around and looked at the room where she sat alone. A bachelor's paradise, she thought, filled with video games, a pool table, and a dartboard.

She hopped off the stool and walked to the doorway of the other room. Flipping on the light switch, she cast her gaze over the theater room that would seat twenty people.

Letting out a breath, she turned off the light and walked to the other side of the room where there was a wall of windows looking out to the manicured backyard. There was a hot tub, and beyond that a swimming pool, no doubt heated so that it could be used longer in the year, or so she would assume.

It wouldn't take much to get used to living like that, she thought.

Everything Laura had, she'd earned, because she understood the value of hard work.

Her parents had worked their fingers to the bone to give Laura any sense of normal among her peers. Living in a multi-generational, multi-family home, they made sure they enrolled Laura in good schools, no matter what they had to do to get her there each day.

They'd worked every job they could when they'd come from Mexico. Her mother cleaned houses like the one Laura stood in, and then she'd take in laundry, and make burritos for her father to sell when he went to work with the road crew. And because they worked so hard, Laura went to school in clothes that matched those of her peers, had a new lunch box each year, and she could buy books at the book fairs.

Laura saw their hard work, and it instilled in her a work ethic that made her what she was today. It had also given her a sense of pride in who she was as a person.

Her goal to be successful stemmed as much from the desire to be the best in her field as it did to pay her family back for what they'd given her.

Now, her abuela lived in a retirement community and played cards every day. Her parents lived in the house her mother had dreamed of living in, and her father enjoyed tending to the yard, just as she assumed Toby did.

But no matter her successes, it was nothing compared to what Toby Maxwell had. What would her parents think of him, she wondered.

CHAPTER 11

*T*oby skipped down the stairs to the basement and found Laura standing by the windows looking out over the back yard.

There was something about having someone new in his house, and not even a week ago he'd threatened to have her arrested.

He watched her for a moment. The fancy suit, made casual by not wearing the jacket, dressed the package perfectly, he thought. Though he couldn't imagine she'd normally wear a flowery demi-bra under a thin cami like that.

When she turned from the window, she pressed her hand to her chest. He'd obviously startled her.

"I didn't mean to scare you," he said, tucking his hands into the front pockets of his jeans.

"I was admiring your yard. Do you mow all of that, too?"

Toby nodded. "It's peaceful. Are you ready?"

"The rest of my files are in my car," she said as she crossed the room.

"You can drive. Your car is already in the driveway."

Laura's brows rose. "Okay."

As she passed by him, and ascended the stairs ahead of him, Toby kept his eyes focused only on the next step. The lonely man in him wanted too much to admire the curves of the woman in the suit, but he knew better. He wasn't happy about having to sign papers to allow strangers into his house. He wasn't happy about having a wedding at his house either. And wasn't he still mad that he'd caught her taking pictures without his permission?

Maybe he wasn't as mad as he thought he'd been. No, he was just pathetic.

With all four of the men he called brothers now married, or committing to marriage, and most having had kids, he had been feeling the looming ache of loneliness creeping up on him for a while. It had been a long time since he'd thought a woman was attractive. No, it had just been a long time since he'd taken the time to appreciate a woman.

Laura walked out of the house and to her car. Pulling open the back door, she took her jacket from the back seat and shrugged it on in the August heat. She'd be sure to take neutral undergarments to work to store there in case she were to spill again. And, Laura knew, she would.

Closing the door and opening the driver's door, Laura slid in behind the wheel as Toby climbed into the passenger seat.

"It's ninety degrees," he commented as he looked at her in her suit jacket. "I don't think Sarah will think less of you if you're not dressed in the whole suit."

Laura started the car and turned up the air conditioner. "Let's just say it's more appropriate."

She noticed the way the corners of Toby's mouth curled up slightly as he slid on his sunglasses. Yeah, he'd noticed the bra through the sheerness of the top she wore. Way to make an impression, Laura thought as she put the car in drive and started down the dirt road toward the guest house.

"What made you buy here?" Laura asked as the road turned to dirt and her car bounced along.

"Look around. Who wouldn't want to live among this?" he asked, accentuating his point cranking his neck to look up at the Flatiron mountains that stood erect behind the property, which was seated in a lush valley.

"Where did you live when you were building?"

"Out here, where Sarah and Bruce live."

"It's a nice house."

Toby nodded. "I actually miss it," he said, looking out the window. "There's a simplicity to it."

Laura wondered if the lonely millionaire was simple, like the guest house, or fancy like the big house. He liked his wine and fine things, but he mowed his own lawn.

When the guest house came into view, Laura noticed the small smile that settled on Toby's lips. He appreciated the little house, she decided.

"What will you do when they move into their own house?" Laura asked as she pulled up in front of Sarah and Bruce's.

"I guess things will be as they were. The house will be here for anyone who needs it. I'll come down from time to time when I need to clear my head." He shrugged as she put the car in park. "My parents will visit. My brother will come and use it when he comes to fish."

"That sounds nice. You're close to your family?"

Toby nodded. "I am. It's hard being away from them, but it's the norm now, and I have the guys. They've always been my family."

"I look forward to meeting them all," she said, and she found that she honestly meant it.

"Why don't you come by on Sunday, we're having brunch and you can meet everyone after our basketball game."

"You have a basketball game?"

He chuckled as he took off his seatbelt. "Every Sunday

morning at the YMCA. We were all on a team in college. Craig married Coach's daughter. Alex married her best friend. Ray is re-married to his college sweetheart, and Bruce has done the unthinkable, and shacked up with Alex's little sister," he laughed now. "They're my family too."

Laura watched as he spoke. He loved each and every one of the people he mentioned, she could see that in his eyes.

"I'd love to meet them at brunch," she said.

"It's a date." Toby opened the car door and stepped out onto the gravel.

Laura took a moment and collected herself. She now had multiple dates with the man in one week. What the hell was she doing? He was going to have her arrested and now he was inviting her in.

Her mind was being pulled from her business, and no one had ever done that to her before. She was going to need to get a hold of herself. Watching Toby skirt her car and stop as if he was waiting for her, she let out a breath. All she wanted from the man was the use of his house. She needed to remember that, because she was sure she could fall for the lonely millionaire, and she didn't have time for that.

CHAPTER 12

*T*oby waited as Laura gathered her things. When she stepped out of her car, he slowly started walking toward the front door with her only a step behind.

As they approached, the front door opened, and Sarah stepped out onto the porch in a short pair of shorts and a tank top. Her hair was piled atop her head and she fanned herself with a piece of cardboard.

"Hey," she said. "Did you come to fix the air?"

Toby blinked hard behind his sunglasses. "What's wrong with it?"

"It's not working. I swear it's over a hundred in the house."

"I'll make a phone call. When did this happen?" he asked.

Sarah laughed. "A few hours ago. We texted and called."

Toby pulled his phone from his pocket and noticed the missed calls and texts. "Sorry. I was out mowing the lawn," he admitted as he scrolled through the contacts in his phone. "I'll get someone out here as soon as possible."

Sarah walked down the steps toward them. "I didn't expect to see the two of you coming out here together."

It was then he realized it must have been a bit odd for them to have shown up in Laura's car together, and by the way he was dressed, he didn't look as if he'd been mowing the lawn.

Laura walked toward Sarah with her files in her hand. "I needed to get some things signed by Toby, for use of his house, and my financial department notified me that I forgot to collect your deposit."

Sarah's eyes went wide. "Oh, goodness. We even talked about that," she laughed and Laura reciprocated as she delicately wiped away a bead of sweat on her brow. "C'mon in. I'll get you something to drink and I'll get you a check."

"Thank you," Laura said as she followed Sarah into the house.

Toby looked down at his phone. "Where's Bruce?"

"He's out back," Sarah said. "He was looking at the air conditioner unit."

Toby nodded. "I'll walk around."

As Sarah and Laura walked into the house, Toby walked around to the back of the house where Bruce stood over the air conditioner.

Toby watched as Bruce stared at the metal box, as if he were simply wishing it to come back to life.

"Are you whispering to it?" Toby teased and Bruce lifted his head.

"Tell me you're here to fix this damn thing."

"I just sent a text to my guy to have him come out A.S.A.P."

"Good," Bruce said as he stood and wiped the back of his hand over his brow. "I'm seriously considering a hotel for the night. Or maybe even going to my grandmother's."

Any other night, Toby would consider inviting his friends to stay at his house. Tonight, though, he'd invited Laura back for dinner. He still wasn't sure that was a wise idea, but he'd done it.

"I suppose if you were to spend the night at your grandmother's house, you'd eat well," Toby offered.

Bruce chuckled. "That is true. What are you doing out here if you're not here to fix this?"

Toby tucked his hands into his front pockets. "I rode out with Laura."

Bruce's brow rose. "The wedding gal?"

"Seems as if she forgot to get your deposit."

"Planning a wedding ensures you're broke going into your life together," Bruce teased. "But don't tell Sarah I said that. If she doesn't get to have kids with me, then the least I can do is make sure she has the fanciest wedding ever. And I owe you for letting us use your house."

Toby wasn't excited to have people in his house, but hearing Bruce talk about the wedding, and Sarah getting what she wanted out of it, Toby knew it was the right thing to do. Besides, he'd secured himself a few dates out of it too, well, if he looked at it that way.

Laura was going home with him for dinner, and they were driving to Palisade on Wednesday. That, he decided, was a bit more than a date. That was hours in a car together where neither of them could escape.

It was then Toby felt the heat.

"Want a beer?" Bruce offered.

Before Toby could answer, Sarah and Laura walked out onto the back porch. Toby noticed that Laura had taken off her jacket, but held it over her arms, in front of her chest.

"I'll pass for now," he said as he looked up toward the women. "Did you get everything taken care of?"

Laura nodded. "I did. Thank you."

"We'll head back then." Toby turned to Bruce. "My guy should be here in the next two hours. If you want, I'll put you up somewhere."

Bruce shook his head with a smile. "We could head out for dinner if it'll only be a few hours."

"Let me know if it doesn't get fixed. I promise to get it taken care of."

Bruce rested his hand on Toby's shoulder. "You do enough for us. We can get through this. You continue your evening, and I'll talk to you tomorrow."

There was a knowing glimmer in Bruce's eye, and Toby didn't much like that. He wasn't sure what had prompted him to invite Laura to stay for dinner in the first place. Signing her contract and sending her on her way would have been the smarter move. Instead, he'd invited her in, poured her a glass of wine, offered to take her to Palisade, and share his dinner. Maybe the flowery demi-bra did more to him than he had thought.

"Thank you for your understanding," Laura's voice broke through Toby's thoughts and he looked up to see her extend her hand toward Sarah's. "I usually have all my ducks in a row. Saturday was a busy day, and, well, thanks for understanding."

Sarah shook Laura's hand. "Oh, if I don't have a sticky note attached to the back of my phone, the fridge, or my mirror, I forget everything," Sarah laughed. "I look forward to stopping by next week and looking at invitations."

Toby heard the groan from Bruce and he chuckled. Yeah, it was worth letting them use the house just to watch him squirm, Toby thought again.

CHAPTER 13

*L*aura opted to leave her jacket off. She'd draped it over the backseat, before she climbed into her car and started the engine. Luckily, the air was cooler than it had been in Sarah's house.

Toby slid into the passenger seat and closed the door. "That didn't take too long," he said, as he fastened his seatbelt.

"Thank goodness. It was too hot to stay there much longer."

Toby's phone chimed and he pulled it from his pocket and looked down at it. "I just got a text. My guy is already on his way."

Laura put the car in reverse and backed away from the house. "Are you *that guy*? The one who has a guy for everything?"

As Laura put the car in drive, Toby slipped on his sunglasses. "You say *that guy* as if it's a bad thing."

"I didn't mean it like that." She took a moment. "I'm sorry. That did seem a bit condescending. I guess, in my own life, I'm *that gal*." Now she chuckled.

"You have an HVAC person on speed-dial?"

"HVAC, plumber, electrician, dry-cleaner, carpet-cleaner, seamstress, florist, printer, and the list goes on and on."

Toby smiled at that. "We're more alike than I thought."

"It's the business thing, right? I mean, you have to have people to run a business." Laura eased the car over the uneven terrain of the dirt road. "I have to have people I can rely on at a moment's notice."

"I agree. And I make sure to take care of those people," Toby agreed.

"Right." Laura shifted a glance his way and smiled. "The Cookie Depot on Pearl Street, they're great for gift giving if you ever need to send something to one of your go-to people."

"I'll look them up," he said, grinning.

Part of being in business was the incessant need to network, and Laura Torres was a master, he decided. And hadn't he done the same without even thinking about it? After all, they were headed to Palisade on Wednesday to taste wines that she might be interested in.

As his house came into view, he wondered if he should offer to find a place for them for Wednesday night. A day of wine tasting shouldn't be followed by a four-hour drive back home. Then again, it might be presumptuous of him and she might not appreciate that. And with more thought, maybe he should cancel dinner and let her go on her way. She had to have more to do than sit at his house any longer than she needed to.

"I was thinking," she said, again interrupting the negative dialogue in his own head. "Maybe we should get a place to stay on Wednesday. I'm a bit of a lightweight, and wine goes right to my head."

Toby chuckled. "I was just thinking the same thing."

"You've been really generous this week with the house, offering the trip to the winery, and dinner tonight. I'll take care of the arrangements to stay overnight. If that works for you. I know you have a busy schedule."

Toby thought about the meetings he'd have to reschedule, and the site walkthrough as well. At that moment, none of it mattered, and that bothered him. But he nodded in agreement. "I think staying is the right choice."

"I'll get that arranged first thing in the morning," she said as she pulled the car into the driveway.

This was his opportunity to send her on her way, he thought, but he couldn't do it.

"How do you like your steak?"

Laura sat on the patio, a glass of wine in her hand, and a breeze from the mister keeping her cool as Toby grilled their steak. A part of her wished she'd had a gym bag in her car so she could change out of her suit, which would need to be cleaned simply because of the heat.

She hadn't given much thought to her bra showing through her top since they'd arrived back at his place. Even though he was being kind with his invitations, Laura wasn't so sure she'd won over the lonely millionaire. At any moment she was sure he'd still threaten to call the police on her.

"How long does it take you to mow this yard?" she asked, looking out over the lush green lawn.

Toby lifted his gaze from the steak to the yard. "A few hours every week."

"And you don't mind it?"

He shook his head. "I'm sure you have something that you do to take your mind off of your work. Mine is yard work."

Laura sipped her wine and gave it some thought. Sundays were her only days off of work, usually. She filled the day with grocery shopping, house cleaning, laundry, and dinner with her parents and grandmother. Were those her mind-numbing activities that kept her from thinking about work? How sad was that?

Toby flipped the steak. "I also play basketball with the guys on Sunday mornings."

"Every Sunday?"

"If I'm lucky, it's every Sunday."

Laura watched him pick up his wine and take a long sip. There was something about the Sundays playing basketball that made him emotional.

"And this Sunday you're going to have them over for brunch too?"

He nodded. "We'll eat out here." Toby looked out over the yard. "Ray's kids love the pool, and the other kiddos can, I don't know, sit on a blanket on the grass."

"They're all very little?"

"Very."

"And that makes you nervous?"

Toby shrugged. "I've never been around kids much. Ray's kids are old enough to do things on their own. Babies, that's a different story. What about you?"

Laura stood, wine glass in her hand, and walked toward Toby. "I lived in a house with my parents, grandparents, two aunties and their families. Babies were part of my upbringing."

"And now how do you feel about them?"

Laura sipped her wine. "About my cousins or babies in general?"

His eyes went wide before they settled on hers. "Babies in general."

"I think they're cute."

"Ever think about having one?"

Laura swallowed hard as they seemed to be locked into one another's gaze. "I think about having many of them."

She watched him process that without blinking. What in the hell had they just stumbled into?

CHAPTER 14

*D*on't forget Sunday brunch after basketball. Toby sent the text out to his friends on Tuesday morning as he sat in his car waiting for those on Bruce's corporate team to pull into the vacant lot.

Everyone responded with an RSVP of sorts.

Bruce was the first of his team to arrive, and he pulled in next to Toby. As soon as he turned off his car, both men stepped out onto the gravel and walked toward one another.

Bruce looked at the text on his phone, and then adjusted his sunglasses. "Brunch. I forgot we'd talked about that," Bruce admitted. "Just the regular gang is going to be there?" Bruce's brows rose as he asked.

Toby had expected this. He knew that Sarah and Bruce had driven by the house while Laura's car had been there. And when they'd returned home last night, after the air conditioner had been fixed, her car had still been there too.

"What does it matter?"

Bruce shrugged, but the grin on his face said he wasn't quite done with Toby.

"Spill it, dude. Last week you were throwing my wedding

planner off your property, and as of last night you're..." he paused for effect.

"As of last night I shared my steak with her."

"And that means?" he continued to draw out his words.

"You're immature."

"Completely. And you're never involved. So, now I'm curious."

"It means I had a steak in the refrigerator. I asked her to stay and share it with me. We had a bottle of wine, played a game of pool, and watched a movie."

Bruce nodded slowly, that stupid grin still tugging on the corners of his mouth. "And she got up and went to work at what time this morning?"

"Grow up."

"I'm all grown up, friend. This is how it works in the adult realm."

Luckily, the other cars began to pull into the lot, and Toby hoped he was done answering Bruce's childish questions.

As everyone began to file out of their cars, Toby opened the back of his and took out his hard hat and his notebook.

Maybe he was irritated with Bruce because he didn't have anything to tell him. They'd eaten, played that game of pool, and watched an old Clark Gable movie in his theater room while eating ice cream.

When that was over, they both deemed that Laura was sober enough to drive home. And that had been that.

Of course, just thinking about her had kept Toby up all night. The very thought that he'd be spending the next two days with her sparked an energy in him that would get him through the day.

The last thing he needed to be doing was getting involved with Sarah's wedding planner. But she intrigued him—a lot.

Then again, they were like-minded spirits. They understood throwing yourself into your work and only having time for family, and for Toby, the team was his family.

The trip to the winery would be networking for her business. And even brunch on Sunday would be Laura's opportunity to meet the others who would be part of the wedding. It all made sense.

And for the rest of the day, Toby would continue to repeat those things just to convince himself that it was all about business and nothing else.

~

Laura sat in the design room and looked at the planning board for Sarah and Bruce's wedding. A picture of Toby's house was pinned in the center of the board, and a card with the date December twenty-sixth.

Sarah would be coming in that following week to pick out invitations, and from there, it was full steam ahead.

Laura twirled her gold pen between her fingers. She needed to ask Toby what kind of decorations he used during the holidays. The house was probably magnificent at the holidays. But with the right amount of lights, and an enormous Christmas tree in the front windows, that was two stories high, that would be a sight.

Leaning back in her chair, Laura thought about the evening she'd spent in the house with Toby.

They'd found comfort in talking about business. Though tech and wedding planning were completely different, the mindset of an entrepreneur had its similarities.

And for Laura, everything was about business. The wedding she was currently obsessed with, was business. The house in the valley, surrounded by the mountains, it was business. The lonely millionaire who could introduce her to the owner of a winery—it was all business.

Squeezing her eyes closed and then opening them, Laura shook any thoughts of Toby Maxwell out of her head. There were eight more weddings happening before the Burke/Griffin wedding. And though the venues didn't have her all twisted up, they demanded her attention too.

"Hey, Laura," Irene poked her head into the room. "You emailed me last night and said you'd be gone on Wednesday and Thursday?"

"Yes."

"The Bradshaw/Court wedding has final fittings on Wednesday."

"Yes, they do."

Irene nodded slowly. "And what do you want me to do with that?"

This was where Laura felt the tension build in her shoulders. This was why she'd built the best team in the business. So why was Irene even asking?

"I want you to move it to someone else's schedule and see that it gets taken care of. I'll be gone all day Wednesday and all day Thursday."

Irene typed the notes into her iPad. "Amy should be fine to take that. And the cake tasting on Thursday?"

"It's all laid out in my email."

Irene smiled and disappeared down the hall.

Their drive to Palisade was only supposed to be for business, but Laura thought now it was turning into two days of self care. She never took time away from her work, and it was harming her business. Her team needed to know they could do it on their own. She had faith in them.

Standing, Laura walked back to her office, closed the door, and sat down at her desk. On her computer screen was an enormous house that reminded her of Toby's. It sat butted up to the mesa in Palisade, and they had reservations to stay there Wednesday night. A quaint bed and breakfast with four rooms, beautiful gardens, a hot tub, and a private patio for each room.

There had been exactly two rooms still available, and Laura had booked them.

Surely Toby needed a few days away from work too. Maybe they could make a pact to turn off their cell phones and forget about the rest of the world.

The thought made her laugh. Hadn't they talked in length over dinner about how tied to their work they were?

Picking up her phone, she scrolled through her contacts until she came upon Toby's name, and the picture of his house. They'd exchanged phone numbers and email addresses over a pint of ice cream while watching an old movie in his theater. They'd even followed each other's businesses on Instagram.

I booked us two nice rooms at a bed and breakfast that looks like heaven. I sure could use a break from work. I'm sure you could too.

Setting her phone back on its stand, she was surprised when it buzzed almost immediately with Toby's reply.

I'll pick you up at your office at nine. And yes, I could use it too.

CHAPTER 15

Toby pulled up in front of the old Victorian house. He put the car in park, pulled off his sunglasses, and stared at the elegance.

The wooden carved sign that hung out front said *Laura Torres Weddings* and was trimmed in gold. The house was as white as a wedding dress, and roses bloomed on trellises against the wrap-around patio. Any woman would go nuts over the house with its white pillars and shutters.

The windows were modern, and the front door boasted an etched, frosted glass that was exquisite. Laura Torres knew fine things, just like she knew her wine.

Toby stepped out of his car and headed up the stone front walk. The porch had been redone in that faux wood that was made of plastic, but from the street no one would have ever known.

He paused as he reached for the front door. Was he supposed to knock or just enter? It was then he saw the small sign by the doorbell that said *During business hours, please enter*.

Pushing open the door, Toby grinned when he saw the modern office space behind the facade of the glorious house.

All of the walls were glass, and he could see into every room and every office. A younger woman hurried toward the door with an armful of lace.

"Hi," she greeted him. "Can I help you?"

"I'm here to see Ms. Torres."

The woman nodded. "Follow me. I'll take you back."

Toby walked down the hallway to what might have once been where a bedroom sat, but now the room was filled with boards full of pictures and samples of napkins and invitations. In the center of the room was a large table. In the middle of the table were stacks of enormous books, which looked like the scrapbooks his mother used to make.

It took him a moment to see the woman in the corner in front of a small computer screen, a telephone receiver held to her ear, and her back turned to the door.

"She'll be right with you," the young woman whispered.

Toby nodded, and stepped into the room. He wouldn't have known the woman in the corner was Laura. Her hair was down and it cascaded in curls far past her shoulders.

The ends of her hair were blonde. Again, something he hadn't expected, as she'd always worn her hair in a bun, obviously to keep that professionalism.

While she talked on the phone, Toby looked at the boards set up around the room. There were names, fabric swatches, dates, and checklists. Surely there was a matching board on a computer too. There was no way anyone still ran a business just on boards and notepads alone.

He saw the board with Sarah and Bruce's names on it, and of course a picture of his house.

December twenty-sixth, he noted the date. He'd have to have his family fly in if they wanted to share the holiday with him, he supposed. But no one deserved a grand wedding more than Sarah and Bruce, so he'd stick around for it.

Toby heard Laura finish her call and hang up the phone. She

sat for a moment, and then pulled a tissue from a box and dabbed it to her face.

Since she hadn't turned yet, he began to feel uneasy about standing there. Turning to leave the room and wait outside, he stopped when Laura said, "Hi."

Toby turned around and saw the face of a woman who absolutely needed a few days off.

"Hi," he said back. "Everything okay?"

Resigned to him seeing her tears, Laura wiped the tissue under her eyes again. "Yeah. Everything will be fine. My bag is in my office."

She stood and walked toward him as if she'd walk right by, but Toby touched her arm and stopped her.

"We can do this another day," he offered.

"Today is the best day to do it," she said, her lips curling into a smile. "C'mon. I'll get my things and we can go."

Toby followed her to the next glass-enclosed room. There was no clutter in her office. Her desk was a dark cherry with a matching credenza behind it. There were a few books, a vase, and an award of some kind displayed. And one single picture sat on a shelf, but that picture must have had thirty people in it.

"Is that your family?" he asked.

Laura turned to look at it. "My abuela, my parents, my aunties, uncles, and cousins."

"No siblings?"

She didn't answer out loud, but simply shook her head.

"I guess you didn't need any. You're all still close?"

Now the worried look on her face changed, and her red-rimmed eyes brightened. "Very close. In fact, so close that when I told my mother I was going out of town on business, with a man, and then also that I wouldn't be at lunch on Sunday, this is what happens." She wiped at her eyes again.

Guilt punched into Toby's gut. "We're only going on business."

"I told her that."

"And you don't have to join us for brunch. Hell, you're going to have plenty of time to meet everyone."

Laura shook her head. "Guilt is a mother's special gift, don't you agree?"

Toby gave it some thought. Yeah, his mother could shell it out with the best of them.

"Seriously, I don't want to cause any problems," Toby admitted.

Her eyes softened as she picked up her weekender bag. "Maybe this weekend I'll meet your friends, and next weekend you can meet my family."

"Now I think I might cry," he admitted and it made her laugh —though he wasn't sure it had completely been a joke on his part.

"My abuela makes the best tamales in Colorado."

"Do you take people to your family meals a lot?"

Laura shrugged. "If someone has time, I invite them. Everyone can use a dose of family from time to time."

Aside from the men he called his brothers, he didn't spend time with his family, though that was just geography.

"I suppose we should see if you still enjoy my company after the next two days."

"If you promise not to have me arrested, I think we'll do okay."

She winked at him as she walked past him and out the door, but the jab had stung.

CHAPTER 16

*T*oby had opted for the convertible for the drive. He didn't drive it as often as he'd like to, but a road trip through the Rocky Mountains warranted it.

Laura had pulled her hair into a ponytail to keep it from blowing, and for the first time since he'd met her a week ago, he thought she looked relaxed.

They'd settled on some yacht rock playlist, though it was hard to hear the music with the sound of the road.

Toby realized, as he took the next curve around another mountain, that he'd been holding a lot of stress in his shoulders. Today, however, he felt at ease. And wasn't that a funny thing to feel when he was spending quiet hours with a woman he didn't even know.

As their journey took them further into the Rocky Mountains, the air cooled. He was sure they'd have to pull over and put the top up, but as he was enjoying it, he'd wait until Laura made the decision.

When they crested Vail Pass, and started their descent into the valley, Toby noticed Laura's head turn, and her eyes lifted to the trees. She was looking for those houses she spoke of that hid on the hill, but sparkled in the sunlight.

Surely he knew someone who had a house up there that he could take her to.

Toby gripped the steering wheel tighter. That wasn't necessary, he thought again. Wasn't this trip to Palisade enough? God, he needed to get a grip. Two people who worked as hard as he and Laura did, they didn't take day trips or vacations—or get involved with others.

"There's a little market up here in the valley. I thought we could stop and get something to eat," he offered.

"I'd like that," Laura said as she pulled out her phone and looked down at it.

Her thumbs moved across the screen on her phone, rapidly texting, before she set it back down on her lap. A muscle twitched in her neck as she eased against the seat.

Maybe they should make a pact to turn their phones off.

"Everything okay?" Toby had to ask. They hadn't said but a dozen words to one another in the past two hours.

"My mother was checking in on me. It doesn't matter if you're thirty-three years old, your mother will still worry about you," she said, and finalized the comment with a tight-lipped grin.

Toby knew that to be fact. Hadn't his mother called him nearly every other day for the past decade? She had a specific time, and he'd even worked it into his schedule. There were never meetings at two-fifteen in the afternoons, just so he could take her call.

"Did you tell her you were going on business?" he asked.

Now the grin turned to a smile. "I did. I told her all about the wedding at your house, and the couple getting married, and that you had an interest in the winery and were taking me to see it."

"And she's worried?"

Laura rolled her head to look at him. "I'm driving four hours in a car with a man that she doesn't know, and I will be staying overnight. She sees a problem with that. She's very—traditional," she gave thought to the word.

Toby made an O shape with his lips and left it at that.

But Laura seemed to have more to say about it as she bounced in her seat to get comfortable again. "I can't imagine she thinks I'm some pristine virgin," Laura blurted out the very private information and Toby wondered if his face had gone red. Not that he judged any woman on that status.

Laura gritted her teeth. "I am a very successful woman. I think I'm fairly attractive," she added and Toby found that caused him to look at her, and then back at the road quickly. "Men take me places—just not often. No one has turned my head enough to make me want to marry them, but it's as if that's the only thing my mother expects and will accept. And, we're going on business. Why does she assume that I'm going to do something *disrespectful* to her?"

Laura tossed her hair over her shoulder and continued her rant. "If I found the right man, that would be one thing. But I'm too busy, and I happen to be in a business where most of the men are unavailable."

That caused Toby to laugh. "I'm sorry. I hadn't thought of it that way."

Now she laughed too. "The groomsmen are more interested in hooking up with the bridesmaids, if it's that kind of wedding."

"If it's that kind of wedding? Do you have a lot of weddings like that?"

"Wedding sex weddings?"

Toby choked and coughed as he laughed. "Yes."

"Yes." She blew out a breath. "But I have a lot of weddings that are about family and the joining of families. Those are the ones that last and create even more beautiful memories down the road. I think Sarah and Bruce will have that kind of marriage."

Toby eased in his seat as he began to steer them from the

highway. "I think you're right. Kids or no kids, they'll have each other, and all of us."

When Toby parked in front of the market, he took the opportunity to lift the top back onto the convertible. Laura hadn't asked him to do so, but she would probably be more apt to ask to have it down than up. If she did ask, he'd put it back down.

They both climbed from the car and walked slowly toward the market.

"Can I ask you a question?" she said as she draped her purse across her body.

"Sure."

"You said something about Sarah and Bruce, with or without kids. They've made similar comments, and that's why Sarah is having an enormous wedding."

Toby knew what she was going to ask and he bit down on the inside of his cheek giving himself a moment to form his answer to the question she hadn't even posed yet.

"Why won't they have a family?" As they neared the market, she reached for his arm. "And you don't have to tell me if you don't want to. Or don't think I should know. I'm a stranger, and I get that."

The wind had mussed her ponytail, and a strand of hair hung over her forehead. Toby couldn't help himself when he lifted his hand to brush it away and tuck it behind her ear.

He noticed her lips part when he did so.

Swallowing hard, Toby took a moment to gather his answer as he looked into her dark eyes, speckled with gold.

"Bruce can't have kids," he said, deciding that the answer should suffice.

"Oh. That's terrible."

"I think they've made their peace with it. They could always adopt, and I've offered to *help*," he choked out the word, "if they want."

Laura's eyes went wide. "That's quite a thing for a friend to offer. They must mean a lot to you."

"Bruce and Sarah? They mean the world to me. They all do. All of the guys, their wives and their kids. They're the best family any man could ever ask for."

CHAPTER 17

*E*ven though Laura grew up in a house filled with family, and family was in her business, personal and otherwise, all the time, she found that she envied the way Toby talked about his friends.

She hadn't spent a lot of time with Sarah or Bruce, but they too had spoken of the group of friends they all shared. What a wonderful asset to have in life, Laura thought as she looked at herself in the bathroom mirror of the little market.

Pulling her hairbrush from her purse, she took her hair out of the ponytail and brushed it. Toby had put the top back up on the car, so she'd leave her hair down now.

As she tucked the loose strands of hair behind her ear, she thought of Toby doing the same thing. It had been such an intimate gesture.

She closed her eyes tight and took a breath. What was she really doing driving to Palisade with him? Laura opened her eyes and looked at herself in the mirror.

His house. She wanted to entertain in his house. Wasn't that it? Hadn't that been it? Didn't she have a notebook full of ideas and drawings of just how she'd use the space that she'd imagined was beyond that manicured front yard?

Toby was a lonely man who was simply occupying himself by taking her on this trip. It was business—only business, just as she'd told her mother it was. Laura had to remember that, she cautioned herself. Because she was lonely too, and it was dangerous for two lonely workaholics to get involved.

When the bathroom door opened, and another woman walked in and ducked into a stall, Laura dropped her brush back into her purse. Why she'd even been thinking about Toby's gesture at all was a mystery.

He had a stake in the winery she was on her way to tour. Any business she did with the winery padded Toby Maxwell's bottom line, and knowing he had multiple fancy cars, a mansion, and a campus for his business, she knew he had to be only about padding that bottom line. More than likely he was taking advantage of her and it was his way of getting back at her for trespassing.

He hadn't had her arrested, but hitting her pocketbook would give him the same satisfaction, she assumed.

Laura pushed back her shoulders and gave herself one last look in the mirror.

There was no need to confuse those two things further. This trip was to pay for Toby's ego, she considered, and the wine would also add to her own bottom line when it was all over.

Toby sat at one of the little tables outside of the market and laid out the two sandwiches he'd purchased and the bag of chips. He wasn't sure what she'd want to drink, so he'd ordered them each a lemonade and bought bottles of water as well.

When he glanced up, Toby saw Laura walk out of the bathroom, look around, and then head his way. She'd taken her hair down, and didn't those curls cascading over her shoulders make her even prettier?

He winced at the thought. This wasn't the time to be thinking like that, especially when Laura's mother already had her antsy with comments about her being with him.

Laura walked through the door as three more people walked in. "It looks like we got here just in time," she said, and Toby nodded in agreement.

"This little market is always busy."

Laura sat down across from him. "Do you come up here a lot?"

"Every month or so."

She picked up a chip and held it at her lips. "An investor wouldn't visit the business every month or so. You have a bigger interest in it than that, don't you?"

Oh, she was good. "I like to keep my finger on each of the businesses I invest in."

She nodded slowly. "You have a say in this company though, don't you?"

Toby leaned in on his elbows. "Maybe I do. You still want to go though, right?"

"More than anything."

"You had me worried," he grinned, picked up his sandwich, and took a bite.

"Business is business." She picked up the sandwich he'd placed on a napkin for her. "Would you really have a baby with Sarah?"

Toby found that the question caused him to choke on the bite he'd taken. He coughed and picked up his lemonade taking a big swig from the straw.

"Sorry, I didn't expect that," he said as he wiped his mouth with his napkin.

"I tend to be a bit direct."

He could have figured that by the way they'd met.

Toby cleared his throat. "Yes, I would really have a baby with

Sarah. Though, it wouldn't be like that. I'd donate to the cause. She'd carry the baby and the baby would be hers and Bruce's."

"But you're part of their lives. The baby would really be yours and Sarah's."

He wondered now why he'd mentioned it. "And I'm sure that's why I wasn't taken up on my offer."

"But they're not married yet."

"And I don't think they'll take me up on it after the fact either."

"But you don't know."

"No, I don't," he admitted.

"You're squirming," she grinned behind her sandwich as she lifted it to take a bite.

"You're a ruthless businesswoman, aren't you?"

Laura winked. "Just keeping you on your toes."

"How am I doing?"

She shrugged. "I suppose you're holding your own." Laura set her sandwich down and took a sip of her lemonade. "So why can't Bruce have kids?"

This time, Toby had taken a littler bite and he was grateful to not have choked.

"You are direct."

Laura smiled. "I am."

"Maybe you should ask them these questions."

"Maybe. But I have you right here." She took another sip of her drink. "And why do they look so familiar to me? When I met each of them, I was sure I'd seen them before. I don't know if they've been in or at weddings I've done. Maybe I've seen them around town. But I know their faces."

Toby winced and pushed his sandwich away. "Why don't we drive while we finish this."

Laura looked down at the sandwich she'd only taken a few bites of. "I'm fine to stay here."

Toby looked around at the people coming and going. "I'd feel more comfortable not being around others."

Laura watched as he began to pack up their lunch so they could carry it to the car and eat it.

She wondered what she'd stumbled on and why Toby had become so flustered. Laura helped gather what was left on the table, and then followed Toby to the car.

For the first time in a very long time, Laura worried that she'd crossed a line with someone and she couldn't fix the situation, and she wasn't sure what she'd said. God she hoped she hadn't blown her opportunity to do more business where Toby Maxwell was concerned. She really wanted to use that house for more than one wedding. The potential could net them both a lot in the end. But her directness might have just put a dent into her grand plans.

CHAPTER 18

*L*aura hurried through the parking lot to keep up with Toby. He'd pulled open the door to the car and slid inside as she juggled her lunch and her drink while she managed with her purse under her arm.

She'd caught his eye, and Laura watched as Toby climbed out of the car and walked around the car to open her door.

"Thank you," she snapped, wondering what in the hell she'd said to make him so jumpy.

Before she could get into the car, Toby touched her arm and stopped her.

"I'm sorry," he said, and Laura watched as a line creased his forehead.

"I didn't mean to…"

Toby shook his head, his hand still on her bare arm, only now he ran his fingers over her skin as if to sooth her.

"It's a touchy subject in which I've been trying to wrap my head around for months."

Laura clenched the purse between her arm and her side harder as to not drop it on the ground and then spill her lemonade. "I'm sorry, I tend to pry. You don't have to tell me anything."

Toby's hand still lingered on her arm and he took a breath as if to consider what he would say next. "You probably do know who Bruce and Sarah are. You probably saw them on the news." He chewed his bottom lip. "Sarah was one of the women abducted by a man who used to work for me, a few months back," he clarified.

The air in Laura's lungs was heavy. She searched her memories to think about news stories in which women were abducted. It only took a moment for her to remember having seen Sarah's face on the news—and Bruce's too. She remembered the news coverage and the face of the man who had taken Sarah. God, she'd watched the series on serial killers where they'd mentioned Bruce's father. Hadn't her mother even kept her up to date on the sentencing of that monster who had not only kidnapped Sarah, but another woman, and killed another.

Laura began to feel sick.

Her hands shook and she was dangerously close to spilling her lemonade.

Laura turned toward the car. She set her lemonade in the cup holder, and dropped her purse and her wrapped sandwich in the seat before she looked back up at Toby. He wore his sunglasses, but she wanted to see his eyes.

Lifting her hands to his glasses, Laura pulled them from his face.

Toby's eyes shifted to the ground.

"I remember them," Laura said and Toby lifted his eyes to meet hers. "The man worked for you?"

He nodded. "I put him on Bruce's team. It was exactly what he'd wanted so that he could get to them. Talk about a sinister plan."

Laura licked her lips. "He killed someone else."

"Sarah's best friend."

The pace of Laura's heart kicked up. "I remember this."

"Considering the back story to it, they've managed to mostly stay out of the news and go on to plan their life together. I suppose it helps that Bruce lived most of his life under another name."

"His father was a serial killer."

Toby nodded.

Laura had remembered watching it all unfold on the news. She'd been with her mother, her grandmother, and her aunt. They'd been terrified and wondered if it had been random. If they turned a corner, would they too become a victim? And to think now, she knew the people who had been affected by that man's hate.

And Bruce—she slowly let out a breath. Did that same kind of hate live within him?

No, she pushed the thought away quickly. In the few times she'd been around the man she didn't feel anything like that resonate off of him. Laura knew love when she saw it, and Bruce was filled with it for Sarah. Sure, he didn't care much about the details of a wedding, but he loved her deeply.

Now Laura rested her hand on Toby's arm. "You take it all personally, don't you? As if it's your fault."

"How could I not? You'd think I'd vet my employees better than that."

She shook her head. "You can't know. People are sneaky." Laura stepped in closer to him, resting her other hand on his other arm and locking eyes with him. "I had a consultant take off with nearly a quarter of a million."

"And you trusted her?"

"With my life," she said then snorted out a laugh. "She was a cousin, so…"

"Ouch."

"Yeah." She let it sting again for a moment, but she'd worked too hard to get past it to let it rattle her now. "You can't let what happened to them destroy you."

Toby shifted, and his hands came to rest on her hips. "It's hard not to."

Because it felt right, Laura pressed her forehead to his. "You need some wine, a nice dinner, a walk in nature, and maybe a soak in a hot tub."

Toby closed his eyes and it was so intimate. Laura's entire body trembled with his hands on her hips, her hands on his arms, and their breath mixing. It was as if they'd kissed, but they hadn't. They were on a business trip, nothing like that was going to happen—just as she'd assured her mother. But they were forging a friendship and building trust.

He had trusted her enough to tell him the secrets of his friends, and share his feelings. She was honored to carry that information.

With her forehead still pressed to his, she took a breath to speak. "He made the decision not to have children, didn't he?"

When Toby nodded, their noses touched. "He didn't want to pass that DNA on to anyone else."

"He's wise."

"Extremely." Toby took in a deep breath, but didn't pull away. "This day took a dark turn."

Laura felt the need to comfort him more, so she took a step forward and wrapped her arms around his neck. "Thank you."

"For what?" he asked as his hands slid from her hips to the small of her back.

"I know I pushed myself into your personal space, and I'm grateful that you're entrusting me with this. I think we're building a friendship here."

"Friendships are nice."

"Especially business ones that could help us both build our worth."

Toby dropped his hands and eased from her embrace. His eyes closed and he stepped back. "You're right. Business friendships are nice. I suppose we should get going."

Laura watched him walk around the car, open the door, and slide inside. She took another moment to collect herself before she picked up her sandwich and purse. Sitting down, she put on her seatbelt, and held the other items in her lap.

Head in the game, Torres. There's no room for romance. Only business.

CHAPTER 19

The rest of the drive had been quiet, after their little interlude in the parking lot.

Toby battled inside of himself between having told Laura about Bruce and Sarah, and just leaving it as fate that she'd find out. He let her stir him up, and then they'd been embracing.

He bit the inside of his cheek as he stewed over the moment their arms were around one another. Oh, but she'd called it—business. It was all business with her, and why was he upset about that. She'd been right. He had initially wanted to have her arrested. Both of their bottom lines would be helped with him introducing her to his business partners. Thinking there was something more to it was foolish. He was so stupid, he berated himself internally.

But, God, she felt good in his arms.

Toby's stomach growled, and it must have done it loud enough that Laura turned in her seat.

"I'd be happy to drive so you can eat. You didn't eat much of your lunch," she said.

For the first time, in nearly an hour, Toby shifted a glance in her direction. "Maybe I'll take you up on that."

"You should. I can handle your car and the mountains. Semi-Colorado native, remember? The mountains don't scare me."

Toby chuckled and eased the car to the side of the highway at the next scenic spot.

When he'd put the car in park, he opened the door and stepped out onto the gravel. Needing to shake out his long legs, Toby walked away from the car and stretched as Laura climbed out of the passenger seat. He kept his back turned to her because he needed to keep his mind focused. Their little episode in the parking lot of the market had him out of sorts.

"What time are they expecting us at the winery?" she asked.

Toby turned, and watched as she pulled her hair back into the ponytail and secured it with the band she'd put on her arm. "One."

"That'll give us enough time to drop our things at the bed and breakfast and change clothes."

He couldn't help but smile. "You're going to change?"

Laura nodded as she put her sunglasses on. "Of course. I can't look like this."

Toby looked at her and he didn't see anything wrong with how she looked. Her toned legs were accentuated by the mid-thigh shorts she wore. And it wasn't as if she wore a pair of gym shorts or cut offs. No, he figured she could walk into any of his board meetings and no one would even realize she was in shorts. There was no doubt that her wardrobe was high end. Even the sleeveless top she wore had a satin sheen to it. And maybe he'd inspected it a little too closely to notice the pattern on the fabric, because he'd been wondering what kind of demi-bra she wore under it.

"For the record, you look amazing. It's very laid back. No one is going to judge your wardrobe."

"I will. I'm here on business. I have to look business-like."

Toby nodded. Well, he could respect that. He too had packed a nice pair of jeans and a button down shirt.

As Laura slid in behind the wheel, Toby stretched one more time. The more business-minded she became, the more he just wanted to get the afternoon over with and get back to his room.

Laura had changed just as she said she would, once they'd checked into their rooms. There was a different feel to being around her when she was in her casual clothes, versus her work suits.

This time she was dressed in slacks and a flowy satin top. A string of pearls had been added, as well as a matching bracelet and earrings.

Her hair was pulled back into the bun she wore when she was all business, and Toby found it hard not to soak in the sight of her as she conducted business.

He had introduced Laura to the owners of the winery, who were dressed in button down shirts and jeans, just as he was. They'd explained their wines—the flavors and notes. She'd asked about their history of wine making and what had drawn them to opening the winery.

Laura understood the process of making wine, Toby noted by her well thought out questions and replies to their questions. They'd taken her through the vineyards and showed her the storage barrels where the wines aged. She was given a bottle directly from bottling, and she engaged with the staff that worked at each area of the winery.

Someday she could be a politician, Toby considered after having watched her shake every person's hand and ask about them personally before asking about their work.

He was learning a lot, he decided. Maybe he'd have known he had a serial killer on his payroll had he dealt with people the way that Laura Torres did.

After their tour, the owners had left them in the private

tasting room, where they had set up bottles, glasses, and an elegant cheese tray.

Though the tasting of wine would be just that, taste it and spit it out, the room was set up for them to enjoy the wine. After all, sales were much better when the customers were plied with a bit of alcohol.

Laura sat on the stool at the table made from an old wine barrel, and she crossed her legs giving Toby a glance at the delicate anklet that she wore.

"Did you arrange the car that picked us up?" she asked as she bit into a cube of cheese, and for the first time he noticed her French manicured fingers as they delicately picked up another cube.

"No, they did that. You're going to be sampling their wines. They're hoping to make a sale. So they want to make sure you get back to your bed and breakfast safely."

Laura nodded as she picked up the first bottle of wine that they would sample.

She read the label, sniffed the wine, and then poured them each enough to get a good taste.

Toby lifted his glass first, taking a sniff before he drank it down. He noticed her watch him carefully. No, he hadn't done the wine service by just gulping it down, but then again, he wasn't the one buying it. He'd already done that.

With great pleasure, he watched as Laura swirled the wine in the glass and watched it. Then she sniffed it again before taking a sip and letting it rest in her mouth until she swallowed it.

"I like this one," she admitted.

"It's the one I had at my house."

She nodded. "I thought so. And rosé is always a favorite at weddings."

They each took a new glass, and this time Toby filled each glass. "This is my favorite," he said as he handed her a glass. "I like the stronger ones."

Laura lifted her eyes to meet his, and his were dark as they looked back at her. Did she understand the sentiment behind that? Had he meant it that way?

Laura repeated the process with the new glass of wine, as she had with the other, and then sipped. He watched as she processed the taste. No, she didn't like it as much, but she had an appreciation for it.

"This one is woody," she said, and Toby took another sip to understand what she was talking about. "I think a variety would be good. Tastes in wine are as different as taste in dresses, flowers, and venues."

"All wedding dresses are different?"

Laura let out a laugh. "Oh my goodness, yes."

"I don't think I'd know if one dress was different from another."

"Then you've never wanted to wear one so badly that you studied every pattern, stitch, or bead."

Toby watched her take another cube of cheese. "What about you? Do you have a dress you've studied?"

There was a playful grin toying with the corners of Laura's mouth. "Oh, yes. I have one."

"Have you bought one?"

Laura shook her head. "No, the dress I always dreamed about can't be bought. It was my mother's and it is the most exquisite dress I have ever seen."

Once they had had a taste from each of the bottles, they agreed to have a full glass and she would consider her order.

Toby poured her a glass of rosé, and he opted for the red.

Lifting his glass to hers, he watched her eyes scan over his face. "To new friendships—business and other. And to new business opportunities, shared between the like-minded."

Toby sat back and drank his wine, but Laura paused, watching him. He couldn't help but wonder what the woman with a flair for business and no time for friends might be thinking. But he was enjoying the moment, having gotten into her head.

CHAPTER 20

*B*efore Laura had placed an order with the owners, which would be shipped to her office, she and Toby had polished off the rosé, eaten the tray of cheeses, and sampled one more glass of the red.

Admittedly, she was surprised she could even sign the order form, promising payment upon shipment. However, all she could hope for was that her nerves of steel covered her intoxication, and she still appeared professional.

Laura shook the hands of each of the men and women who had greeted them, and she watched as Toby did the same, though he hugged each of them as well. Most men in business didn't have that side to them when it came to business, but she was learning he was different.

He took his work seriously and his relationships even more so. More than once he'd spoken about the men he'd gone to college with, whom he called his brothers, and he'd mentioned their coach as well.

Laura wondered what it would be like to have an outside influence, like Toby had with his coach, in her own life. She'd had great teachers, and a few friends growing up. But her life had been molded and shaped by her family. Was it any different, she wondered? Or had it made it harder for her to make friends?

When Laura and Toby climbed into the back of the car which would take them to the bed and breakfast, Laura rested her head back against the seat and placed her hand on her stomach.

"What time did they say dinner was served?" she asked as she closed her eyes.

"Six," Toby replied. "Why don't we stop and get something?"

Laura rolled her head to face him. "I just want to lay down."

Toby smiled and picked up his phone. She watched him scroll and type, then she pulled her phone from her purse and looked at it.

When she chuckled, Toby lifted his head. "What's funny?"

"You suggested we turn off our phones. I did." She stared down at the blank screen. "I can't remember the last time I did that."

"Feels good, doesn't it?"

"It does. Though if the police show up tonight to check on me, don't be surprised. It would be just like my mother to do something like that."

He laughed and turned his attention back to his phone. She watched as he typed some more with his thumbs, then he held down the key on the side, and powered down his phone.

"Now we're both M.I.A."

Laura bit down on her lip. He was something, this lonely millionaire sitting next to her.

Her body had been plied with just enough alcohol that she wasn't only thinking about business, which was rare. Now, she was thinking about Toby Maxwell.

Oh, she'd thought of him since Saturday when she'd walked through his house, taken pictures, and schooled him in pool. But she'd promised herself that he'd be a business acquaintance, and she'd been very good at throwing that into every conversation they shared.

What would happen if she didn't mention it anymore, she wondered. Could he be the friend she'd never had?

"Do you always play basketball at the same YMCA?" Laura asked and Toby turned to look at her.

A small smile crept across his lips. "Yes."

"That must be nice."

"It is. It's something to look forward to every single week. Do you play?"

Laura laughed and then winced when it made her dizzy to do so. Oh, she was going to pay for that indulgence.

"No. I certainly don't play basketball."

"Why not?"

Laura felt a smile tug at her cheeks. "I'm five-foot two. People like me don't play basketball."

"Sarah plays."

"And she has to be nearly six feet tall."

Toby nodded. "She always was better than any of us, and we were some hot shit in our day."

"I'll bet you were all in with the ladies," her words slurred, but she found that she actually didn't care.

"Alex and Bruce were the ladies' men. Ray was already dating Kelly. Craig was always getting caught with Coach's daughter, when she was of age," he added. "I was on the honor roll."

"People on the honor roll get the girls too, you know."

His eyes narrowed on her. "You would have slept with the valedictorian?"

Laura's mouth went dry. "You were the valedictorian?"

Toby raised a brow. "We were too busy to get the girls," he said, without answering the question. "I guess I did okay, though. I mean, I was best friends with Alex Burke and Bruce Griffin. Girls noticed that."

Laura blinked hard. She wasn't sure she wanted to hear any more about Toby and other women.

The car pulled up in front of the beautiful house that had

been made into a bed and breakfast. The thought had crossed her mind more than once, and it was written in that notebook, that Toby's house would make an amazing bed and breakfast.

There were other cars parked out front, and Laura assumed that meant that all of the guests had arrived for the evening.

She hadn't had much time to scope out the house when they'd checked in, but it was such a picturesque setting, she knew it would be one hell of a backdrop for a wedding.

Laura drew in a breath to collect herself. The one thing about drinking wine, she always seemed to feel its effects once it had time to absorb in her body. When her door opened, she winced at the brightness outside. The driver offered his hand, and Laura took it.

She stepped out of the car as Toby climbed out from the other side.

The driver then went to the back of the car and opened the trunk. He took out a canvas bag and handed it gingerly to Laura.

"This is a gift from the winery. Thank you for visiting today," he said.

Laura looked into the bag which had dividers, and four bottles of wine and two glasses.

When she looked up, Toby caught her eye and grinned, then he tipped the driver.

As she wrapped her arms around the bag and started for the front steps, she decided she wasn't going to be any good for anyone tomorrow. Even with her head floating from wine, she knew she wanted to crack open one more bottle, and she wanted to see what the valedictorian had to offer.

CHAPTER 21

*T*oby reached for the bag as Laura wobbled on the first step. She was a lightweight, and he found it endearing. Toby could drink another bottle before he felt the wine.

He offered his free hand to Laura, who took it and giggled. "How much wine did we drink?" she whispered.

"When you figure we drank all our testers and then finished a bottle, a lot."

"I think I get drunker the more I walk."

Toby stifled his laughter. "Wine will do that."

He reached for the front door and they entered the house which smelled of warm cookies. On any other given day, that would have been met with enthusiasm. But even he thought that without food in his belly, the smell of cookies was nauseating.

Their rooms were next to one other, both on the main floor. They stopped outside of her room and Laura pushed open the door.

"I think I'll lay down for a few minutes," she said, stepping into the room then holding on to the door and resting her head against it.

"That's probably a good idea. I'm going to go sit on the patio.

Do you mind if I take one of these with me?" he asked, holding up the bag of wine.

"How come you're not drunk?"

"Practice?" he teased. "Join me on the patio when you're done resting. I arranged for our dinners to be served out there tonight. And they're fixing us a little snack as well."

Laura closed her eyes. "Not the cookies, right?"

"No. Small sandwiches. I texted them from the car."

"I thought you were working."

Toby shook his head. "We said no working, right?"

Laura nodded.

Toby took a step toward his door. "Get some rest. You should open your patio door. Fresh air would do you a world of good."

When Toby disappeared into his room, Laura closed the door. She needed to lay down. Then again, maybe if she took a shower and changed clothes, she'd be more relaxed.

The cool shower shook her from her wine-induced stupor. Laura removed what was left of her makeup and braided her wet hair. Looking in the mirror, she didn't look the professional at all. Maybe that was a good thing. For one, she needed to just be herself around someone other than her family, and maybe Toby wouldn't be attracted to her.

It sounded stupid in her head, but she needed to stay focused, and when she was with him, she was anything but focused. And the more time they spent together, the more that focus wavered. God, hadn't she already decided she was going to drink more wine and see what the valedictorian had to offer?

Yeah, it would be better if he wasn't attracted to her.

Toby sat on the patio that led from his room. A trellis divided his patio from Laura's.

The sandwiches and a small plate of fruit had been delivered to his room. There had been fresh coffee in the kitchen, and he'd filled one of the carafes that they offered to take back to guest rooms. Because he'd hoped Laura would join him, he grabbed two mugs.

Toby sat up straighter when he heard the patio door to Laura's room open. A few moments later, he saw her as she walked around the trellis.

"Hey," Laura said softy.

"Hey," Toby returned as he took in the sight of her.

This was casual Laura, he thought. She was in a pair of shorts that, just like the other pair of shorts, showed off her toned legs. However, this pair of shorts were for comfort, and he had to assume they had been packed for relaxing in her room, and not for him to see.

Her tank top, with its racer back, might have been one she'd wear to yoga, which is where he figured she got those toned arms.

Braided hair fell over her shoulder, and her eyes were even darker when she didn't have makeup on.

There was some satisfaction in seeing her like this. This was raw. This was real, Toby thought.

"We have sandwiches, fruit, and coffee," he offered.

"I could use some coffee," Laura said as she sat down in the chair next to him at the small cafe table. "I hope I didn't embarrass myself in front of your partners."

"Why would you think that?" he asked as he poured her a cup of coffee and handed it to her.

"Thank you," she said as she took the cup. "I completely felt out of sorts in the car."

"Well, you have nothing to worry about. I think you conducted yourself very professionally," he admitted. "They don't usually budge on price."

Laura lifted her cup to her lips and he saw the smile behind it.

"It's just business."

"And they understood that."

She sipped. "I like them. I hope my brides and grooms appreciate the wine."

"I know Sarah and Bruce like it."

Laura set her cup on the table and picked up a sandwich triangle. "If I remember Bruce's story right, his father killed his mother. Right?"

Toby nodded. He hadn't wanted to revisit this story, but until she was comfortable, he figured he'd have to answer her questions. Especially since he didn't want her to feel unsafe around Bruce.

Laura took a bite of her sandwich. Holding her hand in front of her mouth, she asked, "Who will be there for him for the wedding?"

Thinking of the answer had Toby smiling. "His grandmother. Well, the woman who adopted him."

"His grandmother adopted him?"

"The man and woman who took him in were older. They adopted him, but not as his parents. They took on the role of his grandparents."

"That's very sweet."

"They were very patient, from what I understand. You don't take a kid who saw what he did and expect them to not have issues. For what Bruce went through, he's very well adjusted."

Laura contemplated another bite, but looked up at Toby before she bit into the sandwich. "And now? How is he now? How is Sarah?"

Toby watched her take the bite. "They're processing it. He had to face the fact that someone was hurting him and the ones he cared about because his father had hurt them. I wasn't sure he and Alex would remain friends. I mean, it was the reason that Alex had forbidden him to date his sister."

"They mentioned something about that, but I thought it was just a brotherly thing."

"I think we all did until we found out about his dad. Anyway, Bruce went down a dark hole, but we rallied around him, and the love of a woman does a lot for a man," he said.

"How do you work through it?" she asked, and the question had his chest tightening.

"Rachel hooked me up with a therapist. She's a therapist too," he offered. "She knew I'd need to process what happened to my friends and my business."

"That's noble."

"Thank you. I'm trying to learn that."

"Did you say they were going to deliver dinner here to the patio?"

Toby grinned as she changed the subject. "Yes."

"Would you think I'm horrible if I wanted to open another bottle of wine?"

"Are you sure?"

Laura nodded. "With my phone off, and my team having to do the work I trained them to do, I feel like just disassociating and relaxing for a bit. I just don't want to think about being professional right now."

"That's noble," he repeated her earlier sentiment. "Mind if I join you?"

"I wouldn't want it any other way."

CHAPTER 22

*B*ecause Toby's friends at the winery thought of everything, there was a corkscrew in the canvas bag they had given Laura.

Knowing she liked the rosé the best, Toby opened that bottle first and poured them each a glass.

Picking up his glass, he held it out toward Laura. "Here's to disassociating for the night."

"Cheers to that," she agreed before sipping from her glass. "You know what else we need? Music."

"We're going to have to use the clock radio next to the bed, unless we choose to turn on our phones."

Laura shook her head. "The minute we turn on those phones, my mother will call and so will my assistant, Irene. My mother will feel your presence and I will not hear the end of it. And Irene, well, she just loves a little gossip."

Toby chuckled. "Then local radio it is."

Toby stood and walked into his room. He unplugged the clock and carried it back to the patio where he plugged it in and set it on the planter next to the wall. Scanning through the stations, he stopped whenever a sound would come in. Talk radio, weather, classical, and country all crackled on the small radio. When he came to an oldies station, he stopped.

"This is as good as it's going to get," he said.

Laura shrugged. "It'll do." She lifted her glass and took another sip before wandering a look over Toby. "Don't you have anything that's more relaxing to wear?"

"I brought a pair of shorts in case I took a run. Other than that, I only have my swim trunks."

"I didn't think about a bathing suit," she said looking toward the hot tub just beyond the porch. "I guess I'll have to get in in my clothes."

Toby felt the heat rise in his cheeks, and the color pinked in Laura's. Yeah, both of their minds had gone right to them not bothering with swimsuits at all.

Each of them lifted their glasses of wine to their lips and drank.

Two more glasses of wine, and Laura was feeling that buzz she'd been looking for. Business wasn't on her mind at all. In fact, there wasn't anything coherent going on in her mind.

Dinner had been delivered to them, and they continued to sit on the patio enjoying the view and one another's company.

Conversation had steered to Toby's life in Texas, which he thought was boring but stable. The best thing to ever happen to him was the basketball scholarship that sent him to Colorado.

"I don't know if I would have made it all four years without the guys," Toby said as he finished his wine. "I was pretty home-sick when I got here. But they took me in. Craig and Ray had grown up together and roomed together. Alex and Bruce had grown up together, and they roomed together. I was the odd man out with my own room."

Laura filled each of their glasses, finishing the bottle of wine. "You were that guy?"

"That guy?"

"Yeah, the one with their own room. Usually those were the spoiled kids."

Toby chewed his bottom lip. "Spoiled, huh?"

"Sorry. That wasn't nice. But I remember thinking that about the people who didn't have to room with someone."

Toby sipped his wine. "I suppose I was. Though, someone was always in my room. So I can't say that I ever felt as if I had my own space."

With her decorum eased by wine, she set her elbows on the table and watched Toby over the top of her glass. The lonely millionaire wasn't a persona he put on. It was his way of life, she decided. She might have originally been after his house, but her mind, plied with wine, was thinking the energy between them would be fun to explore as well. Then again, hadn't she considered that before the wine?

"Hello?" Toby's voice shook her from her thoughts.

"Sorry, what?" She blinked hard, realizing she hadn't heard anything he'd been saying.

Toby chuckled. "Are you okay?"

"I'm wonderful," she said, hearing her words slur.

"Where did you go to college?"

Laura blinked again, focusing on Toby's dark eyes. "Would you like to dance?" she asked, thinking more about being near him than answering his question.

The smile on Toby's lips told her he was amused by her, and it made him even more endearing. Instead of questioning her, he held out his hand.

Laura took his hand and stood on wobbly legs.

When he pulled her to him, she caught the scent of his cologne, and she was sure it deepened her intoxication.

Toby wrapped his arm around her, pressing his hand to the small of her back as she lifted her arm to drape over his shoulder. Their unoccupied hands clasped together, and Toby pulled them in to press against his chest as they swayed to whatever played on the radio.

For a moment she let the intimacy swirl around her, and she wondered what he was thinking. Laura knew her thoughts weren't pure and business was no longer on her mind at all when it came to Toby Maxwell, the presumed valedictorian.

For the first time since she'd met him, she didn't care about his house and what she could do with it. She didn't care about his connections, or keeping him happy so that Sarah and Bruce's wedding was exactly what Sarah wanted. Laura was only thinking about the man whose body pressed against hers. She was consumed by the man.

Toby's fingers made small circles against her back as he pressed his cheek to the top of her head. This was a dangerous place to be, he thought. He didn't move more than the sway that kept him dancing, but wanted to get closer.

Laura lifted her head, and slowly opened her eyes. Toby slowed their sway and gazed into her dark eyes. There was trust and need—lust and heat.

Their hands which were clasped together, separated.

Laura's hand pressed to his chest, and his came to her cheek. Mesmerized by her slender neck, he brushed his fingers down her delicate skin.

Laura's eyes closed again and her lips parted.

Her fingers gripped his shirt, and in that moment he was lost in that trust and need—in that lust and heat.

Toby lowered his mouth to hers.

Laura's body swayed against his, and her mouth opened to accept his kiss.

She lifted her fingers into his hair, and Toby pulled her closer. Tongues came together, and teeth scraped as they fought to get closer. Their wine-induced connection had them stumbling back to the wall, but their mouths never parted.

Laura's fingers tugged at his hair, and his hands moved from the small of her back and down over the curve of her bottom. She sucked in a breath without breaking their connection.

"Take me inside," she managed with her lips still pressed to his.

It was an invitation that Toby couldn't refuse.

Lifting her to his waist, those toned legs wrapping around him, Toby carried Laura into his room.

CHAPTER 23

*L*aura kept her legs wrapped tightly around Toby's body as he lowered her to the bed. She was afraid to let their lips part—afraid he'd come to his senses.

Her fingers moved to the buttons on his shirt and worked to open them as quickly as possible. There was a need to touch his skin.

When the fabric opened, she pressed her hands to his chest and now she felt him suck in a breath.

This wasn't the first time she'd been in this position, trapped under the willing body of a man she was attracted to. But when her hands came to his skin, her entire body felt the jolt. This was different.

Now she sucked in a breath and Toby eased back, but Laura kept her legs around him.

"I'll be right back," he said softly.

"I'm okay. I'm taken care of. I'm protected," she said with urgency. "You don't have to go anywhere."

The corner of his mouth turned up in a half grin. "I was going to shut the patio door so no one could see us," he said.

"Oh," she said softly as she released her legs from around him and he pushed back off the bed.

As he closed the door, she closed her eyes. The wine swam in her head and in her belly. It would be the perfect excuse to walk away and say it was a mistake. Then again, it was the perfect dose of courage to carry on.

God, this could cost her the wedding she'd hoped for, in the location she'd dreamed about. It could, she realized very clearly, cost her a lot more than that. Toby Maxwell might be soft spoken, but he had a lot of influence in the community in which she did business. He could crush her.

When he passed by the bed, Laura opened her eyes and watched as he locked the door to the room. "Just in case," he said moving back to the bed, and right back on top of her where he'd been moments before.

He didn't kiss her right away. Instead, he lifted her arms above her head and clasped their hands together. The gaze he focused on her was intense, and Laura bit down on her bottom lip to keep it from quivering.

"Are you sure about all of this?" he asked.

Laura nodded.

"I want to hear it. I don't want to stop, but I will. I will at any moment you want to," he promised.

"I'm sure," she confirmed, and his smile was back.

"God, I was hoping you'd say that."

He released her hands, tucked his arms around her, and rolled her so that she straddled him.

Toby steadied her with his hands on her hips. One move and it was going to hurt, he thought, because his body had responded immediately to her straddling him.

Laura locked eyes with him, and the lust that radiated between them made the air in the room thick. He shouldn't be doing this, but he didn't want to stop. Aside from that very moment when he'd first encountered her, there had been a need for her. He didn't understand it. He wanted to hate her for wanting something from him and trespassing into his quiet space, but he couldn't.

They were likeminded, and that was rare to find. And, he knew, they were enough alike to understand when this went south, they needed to continue to be professional. After all, she was part of his life through Christmas, no matter what happened the rest of the night.

Laura lifted her hands to her braid and pulled the band from it. Running her fingers through her hair, she loosened the braid until her hair fell feely over her shoulders.

"You are so beautiful," Toby said as he lifted his hands to the ends of her hair and twirled it around his finger. "You're so elegant in your suits with your hair back. You're stunning in a casual pair of shorts. And you're breathtaking in your yoga clothes with no makeup."

She didn't respond. Instead, she sat, straddled atop him, and stared down at him.

"Should I not have said that?" he asked, letting his hands glide over her shoulders, down her arms, and back to her hips.

"I specifically didn't wear makeup or do my hair, and I wore my yoga clothes so you wouldn't be attracted to me."

Toby chuckled. "You didn't want me to be attracted to you? Why?"

Laura nodded. "It was better if you weren't attracted to me and we didn't' end up like this, because I wanted this to happen."

He took hold of her hands and interlaced their fingers. "I want it to happen too."

"We have a lot to lose," she admitted.

"We don't have to do this," Toby offered. "We can go back outside and sit and drink more wine."

Laura lowered herself so that her hair curtained their faces.

Toby gently ran his fingers up her back, but kept his eyes locked with hers.

She leaned in and pressed a quick kiss to his lips. "I want to do this. I've wanted to do this since I met you."

"That was only a week ago."

"Yeah, well you happen to make an impression," she said.

"So do you," Toby confirmed. "Boy oh boy, do you make an impression."

"I can't decide if I should go back outside and drink wine, or throw caution to the wind."

"I can't make that decision for you, and I will never force my opinion on you."

Laura smiled. "I get very focused on my work," she said as she sat up and his hands went to her hips again.

"So do I."

Taking hold of the hem of her shirt, Laura lifted it up and over her head. Toby sucked in a breath and appreciated the very plain bra she wore.

"Sometimes, I get so focused people think I'm rude, mean, or not interested."

Toby nodded. "I've been told the same."

Laura brought her fingers to the center of the bra, between her breasts, and opened the clasp. As she let the garment fall, Toby's fingers gripped her tighter.

"I'll want more," she informed him as she took his hands and guided them to her breasts.

"I'm not afraid of more, Laura," he used her name and she batted her eyes.

"Then caution is being thrown to the wind," Laura confirmed as she lowered herself to him.

CHAPTER 24

The room had grown dark around them.

Laura rolled from Toby and fell to her back on the bed gasping for air. Toby laughed as he reached for her hand.

"How many hours have we been at it?" he asked through his gasps and laughter.

"I have no idea," Laura admitted as she kissed his fingers. "I do know I'm starving now."

Toby rolled to face her, propping himself up on his elbow. "They did say they always leave out snacks for guests who need a snack in the middle of the night."

"I don't know if I have the energy to walk that far," she said as she turned toward him. Laura lifted her hand to his face and gazed into his eyes. "We should get some sleep. It's going to be a long drive home tomorrow." She picked up Toby's watch and looked at it. "I guess, later today."

"Don't even think about going back to your room to sleep," he said as he rolled himself atop of her.

"I don't have the energy for that either," she professed.

"Okay, then it's settled. You'll sleep in my arms, right here." He lowered his mouth to hers. "But, we can wait to sleep for a few more minutes," he said as he took her under yet again and made her forget there was ever anything else as important as Toby Maxwell.

The bird feeder outside of Laura's office glimmered and captured her attention. Now on her third cup of coffee, she wondered when her usual enthusiasm for her work would kick in.

Their Friday morning staff meeting was in ten minutes, and Laura didn't even care. Her notes were still in her notebook, and her head was in the clouds.

Irene opened the door to Laura's office and walked through with the biggest arrangement of roses Laura had ever seen.

"Why are you bringing those in here?" Laura asked as she set her coffee mug on her desk and stood to cross the room. "Which wedding are those for? I don't remember a rose selection."

Irene's smile grew wider, and Laura noticed Amy and her intern walk past the glass door and look in with smiles as they passed by to the design room for the meeting.

"These aren't for any wedding altar," Irene informed her. "They were just delivered for you."

"For me?"

Irene nodded and handed her the card.

Laura pulled the card from the small envelope. *I can't stop thinking about you,* was all that the card said.

Laura did everything she could to maintain a neutral face, but the smile broke through.

"The house?" Irene asked.

Laura narrowed her eyes and tried to understand what she was asking, but then it came to her. "Yeah, the house," she said, referring to Toby.

"I take it he didn't have you arrested at any point during your evening with him?" Irene asked as she picked up the stack of files that were designated for each wedding they were planning in the next month.

"No. We managed to get along just fine. The winery was nice, and you'll love the wine. I'll give you a bottle when it gets here."

Irene nodded slowly. "I look forward to it. Why don't you get yourself a bottle of water. You're shaking from all the coffee you drank this morning," she noted. "I'll get the meeting organized. You pull yourself together. Our fearless leader has never had stars in her eyes before. Our young protégés won't know how to react," she said with a smile as she let herself out of the office.

Laura looked down at the card in her hand. Toby Maxwell was the whole package. She'd been away from him for exactly four hours, and yet she missed him.

Picking up her phone from the top of her desk, Laura texted him. *The flowers are beautiful. Thank you.*

Before she headed down the hall, Laura finished her cup of coffee.

They'd made it back to Toby's by four o'clock Thursday afternoon. But once again, they stayed up all night making love in every room in Toby's house—or so it seemed. She hadn't fallen asleep until two in the morning, and then she was up at five to go home and get ready.

This wasn't a schedule she could keep. In fact, she was going to have to go home early just to prepare for Saturday's wedding, which was a midday ceremony and evening reception. This, she remembered, was why she didn't date.

I'm glad you liked them, Toby texted back. *Spend the night with me. Come for dinner at 7?*

Laura winced. She couldn't do it. She had to tell him no.

The rest of her staff passed by her office door and each smiled at her, noticing the flowers, as they walked to the design room for their meeting.

I have a wedding tomorrow, she replied.

I'll have you tucked into bed early. I promise.

Laura dropped her phone into the pocket of her suit jacket and then picked up her iPad and notebook.

There had never been a time when Laura couldn't say no to something that didn't serve her. Sleeping in the arms of the man she was having sex with wasn't going to serve her tomorrow morning, that was for sure. Toby was a businessman, and he'd understand the need for her to be on top of her game. After all, each wedding was pure advertising for the weddings still to come —and there were always weddings still to come.

Toby waited for the text to confirm dinner, but it never came. His fingers hovered over the keyboard of his phone wanting to ask again, in case it didn't go through on Laura's end.

The words of past girlfriends continued to float through his head. *"You're needy." "I need some space." "I'll call you when I'm ready."*

Laura didn't appear to be the kind of woman who would tolerate his needy side. If he wanted things to work out, he needed to remember to give her space.

"Lunch today?" Bruce's voice broke Toby's thoughts, and he looked up to see Bruce standing in the doorway to his office.

"Yeah, sure."

"Craig doesn't have any classes today, so he's going to meet us."

Toby nodded and Bruce gave him a thumbs up as he walked away. No one had asked about his night in Palisade yet. And what was he going to tell Bruce when the subject did come up?

CHAPTER 25

*C*raig was sitting at a high top table in the bar of the restaurant when Bruce and Toby walked in.

"I ordered an appetizer," Craig said as they sat down. "I forgot to eat breakfast this morning, and I'm starving."

Bruce chuckled. "I can't recall you ever missing breakfast."

"Angela was fussy this morning. Time got away from me," he admitted as he leaned in and studied Toby. "Time seems to have gotten away from you, too. When did you sleep last?"

Toby looked at Bruce who lifted his brows, then turned back to Craig. "Why do you say that?"

"Because you haven't had dark circles like that under your eyes since senior year. Well, at least you haven't in the past few years. What kept you up so late?"

Bruce chuckled. "It's not what, it's who."

Craig tapped the tips of his fingers together like a mad genius. "Oh, do tell."

Toby shook his head as the server set down three waters and a beer in front of Craig. Bruce eyed the beer and Toby snorted a laugh. "I don't care if you have one."

"Good," Bruce said. "I'll have a beer, and so will he." He

nodded in Toby's direction before the server took off. "Now fill Craig in on your rendezvous."

"Rendezvous?" Toby took the bar napkin on the table and began to fold it into little triangles. "It was a business opportunity."

Craig leaned in closer. "C'mon. Don't make me go fishing here."

Toby pushed away the napkin. "I took Bruce's wedding planner to Palisade to tour the winery. She had some wine at my place and liked it. So we went up so she could see the facility and the vineyard."

"The wedding planner you yelled at for looking at your house?"

"Yes."

"The wedding planner you had at your house on Monday night?" Craig held up his hand before Toby could ask his own questions. "The wives of our circle of friends are as tight as the five of us. Rachel will want to know when you're getting married."

The server delivered their beers. Without looking at a menu, they each ordered lunch. It hadn't been a long enough exchange, Toby decided, when both men had their eyes fixed on him again.

"Don't let Rachel go planning a wedding. Laura and I are just connected because of Bruce's wedding."

Bruce leaned back in his chair. "Yeah, because I'm getting married, he had the wedding planner over for dinner on Monday, drove her to Palisade on Wednesday, stayed until Thursday, and then she spent the night last night," he drew out the last words to emphasize his knowledge on the subject.

Craig puckered his lips. "Well, well, well."

"Who says she spent the night last night?" Toby asked.

Bruce grinned as he picked up his beer and took a sip. "Thursday night, friend. We might not have had guys' night at your house, but we watched the game at Alex's house. And the girls went out for nachos and margaritas."

Toby picked up his beer and waited for the rest of Bruce's story.

"I drove by your place at ten. Sarah drove by your place at midnight. Laura's car was in the driveway the entire night," Bruce explained.

Toby took a long drink from his glass. "Then if you know all of that, you don't need any further gossip from me."

Craig and Bruce offered one another high-fives and chuckled over Toby's confession.

Toby kept his lips tight so he wouldn't smile, but it was hard. He wanted to tell his best friends about the woman he'd been with. God, he'd had more sex in the past forty-eight hours than he'd had since—well, he couldn't remember having that much.

When Laura was around, they couldn't keep their hands off one another. Even sitting there having a beer with his friends, all he could think about was Laura, and how she hadn't responded to his invite.

"I didn't take you for a wham-bam man," Craig admitted as he took a sip of his beer. "I pegged you to be the guy who was friends with a gal for years and years before you got the guts to even kiss her on the cheek."

Toby shook his head. "Thanks for the vote of confidence."

"Okay, so that sounded mean. But I mean, you think things through. You don't rush into things, and you certainly don't jump into bed with people. You met her a week ago," Craig reminded him.

"Things change."

"I guess they do. Actually, I'm proof that they do. Look who I'm married to." Craig chuckled as the server set an appetizer platter in the middle of the table. "Rachel and I had every odd stacked against us. Now here we are. Married with a kid. What would her dad think about that?"

Bruce picked up a cheese stick and broke it in half, letting the cheese drip down to the plate. "He'd be proud as hell of both of you," Bruce said before he looped the stringy cheese around the breaded piece between his fingers. "He'd be proud of all of us."

Toby took a fried pickle and popped it into his mouth. Bruce was right. Coach would have been proud of all of them. Hell, he'd be proud of Toby for not over-thinking a relationship before he jumped into bed with a woman he'd wanted to have arrested.

The thought humored him and he chuckled. Hopefully Laura didn't think he'd been insensitive because things had moved so quickly—and boy had they moved quickly.

Toby pulled his phone from his pocket and checked his messages. She still hadn't returned his text.

She was a busy woman. He'd hold off on texting or calling her, but that was going to be hard to do.

CHAPTER 26

*S*itting back in her office chair, Laura stretched and looked at her watch. It was six o'clock. The last of the items had been loaded into the van in preparation for tomorrow.

Her team would pick up the van early in the morning and head out to the church to get everything ready. Dressing rooms would be outfitted with flowers and champagne. The pews would be decorated to accommodate seating, but to the observer it would appear to be just a decoration.

Before the wedding, cars would pick up the wedding party from different locations, and take them to the church. Hair stylists and makeup artists were scheduled to arrive, and the caterer would also set up a very small table of food, which Laura would convince the bride to nibble on to keep up her strength through her nerves.

Things would go wrong, but Laura and her team would be there to right them. The bride and groom would have the day they dreamed of, and that was Laura's promise.

Laura picked up her phone and looked at her texts. She'd never replied to Toby, and he hadn't texted her again. She supposed that had been a test of sorts.

When the stunning rose arrangement arrived that morning, Laura fought off being mad. It had caused a commotion in her controlled space—the space in which she was the boss. Too many questions had arisen over the flowers, which now scented her office.

She wasn't mad now, but she wasn't going to his house for the night.

I won't be coming over tonight. Tomorrow starts too early. I can leave after the cutting of the cake tomorrow afternoon and spend the evening.

Laura read the text, and reread it. It was a bit curt and she didn't want to appear mad. She just needed to be as straightforward with her new lover as she was with a vendor.

New lover—she thought again. She didn't have time for this. But she was enjoying it. There was something about being so tired because they couldn't keep their hands off one another.

Laura turned off her computer and the lamp on her desk.

Sex wasn't a relationship. Therefore, she convinced herself, the text was fine.

Reading it one more time, Laura added a heart emoji and *XOXO.*

Picking up her bag, she stood from behind her desk, and draped her suit jacket over her arm. Honestly, no matter how much she was enjoying Toby, physically and emotionally, it was all about keeping the peace until Sarah and Bruce's wedding. At least that's what she would continue to say to herself.

I understand. I'll see you tomorrow night. Have a great wedding, he added with a smiley face emoji.

Laura continued to look at her phone, but no more texts came through.

His text had been as to the point as hers had been.

She recalculated her schedule again. Maybe she could—no, she didn't need to be rearranging her schedule for sex.

As she started out of her office, she turned and took a single rose from the vase. Holding it to her nose, she inhaled deeply.

For the first time since she'd opened her business, she couldn't remember a time when she started counting down the moments until she could leave a wedding.

~

Toby opted for a frozen microwave meal for dinner. He'd planned out something much nicer for Laura, but he'd save it for tomorrow's dinner.

As he pulled off the plastic cover, the doorbell rang, and he nearly threw the tray in the trash. She'd had a change of heart, he thought. His heart began to race, and he hurried to the front door.

Without even looking out to see who it was, Toby pulled open the door, and knew he'd looked disappointed enough to find Sarah standing there that she shook her head.

"Sorry that it's me, huh?" she pushed past him and into his house.

He followed her to the kitchen, where she walked straight to the refrigerator, pulled it open, and took out a Gatorade.

She was still dressed from work, so she hadn't been out running or come to use his gym.

Sarah placed the bottle on the island and twisted off the top of the Gatorade. She stared down at it, picked it up, and then contemplated a drink—which she didn't take.

Twisting back on the top, and then twisting it back off before finally taking a drink, Toby was quite sure she was mad.

Bruce must have said something to her that had her fleeing only as far as his house.

After she took a long sip, she set the bottle on the counter, but kept the top in her hands.

"Don't ruin this for me," Sarah spat out the words without looking up at him. "Don't mess up the only normal thing I'm ever going to have."

Toby dared to take a few steps toward the island, yet safely on the opposite side of Sarah. "What am I ruining?"

"My wedding, dammit," she snapped her head up and it was the first time he'd noticed her eyes were red from the tears that welled in them.

"How am I ruining your wedding?"

"By sleeping with Laura."

Toby let out a breath. So, she'd talked to Bruce and this was her reaction. He would have hoped she'd have been happy for him, and for Laura.

"Sarah…"

"I mean it. God, if you break her heart, she'll ruin my wedding."

Toby rested his hands on top of the island. "I seriously don't think she'd do that."

"Because you know her so well now? God, Toby, why her?"

"I don't know," he answered, and he contemplated that. He'd been damn sure he never had wanted to see the woman again. Why he was consumed with her now, he wasn't sure.

"I get a big and elegant wedding. That's all I get that will be normal. And I know that. And I'm okay with that. I love Bruce so much, I'd run away with him and get married." She wiped her tears. "I'll never have my husband's children, and even though you offered, I don't want your kids to make up for it."

That stung, but he understood what she was really trying to say.

As she wiped her tears, and took a breath, he knew she had more.

"I'll move the damn wedding from your house if that's why you're doing this. I mean—why?"

Toby would never consider that he understood women at all, and this little outburst of Sarah's proved it.

"I'm not really sure what you're mad about," he admitted holding up his hand so she would hear him out. "I'm okay with you having your wedding here. I really am. And yes, the woman rubbed me the wrong way when I met her, but now, it's not like that."

"It's been a week, Toby. That's a lot of emotion for you to process in one week."

He wanted to laugh. Sarah had never been one to be overly emotional, so he thought it was odd that she was crying in his kitchen over his sex life.

"Your wedding isn't going to be ruined," he offered and took the chance that she wouldn't punch him, and walked around the island to her. He gathered her hands in his. "I like her. I mean I really like her, and she shuts down my needy side really quickly," he admitted with a chuckle.

"You promise everything will be okay?"

He wasn't sure how he was going to do that, but he nodded. "I'll make sure of it." Toby kissed her cheek. "Is this really all that's wrong? I mean, c'mon, the Sarah I know wouldn't fret this stuff."

Her lip trembled and she bit down on it. "I'm nervous."

"And that's normal."

"It scares me, because I don't want to be nervous. I'm never nervous."

"This is forever."

"But it's with Bruce. That shouldn't make me nervous."

He gave her hands a squeeze. "And you've been through a lot this year. Nerves and fear are going to be heightened now."

She nodded as if she knew that.

Toby wiped away her tears. "Call Rachel. Talk this out with someone who knows and understands. When you have therapy next, address this. And, if it comes down to my sex life being your problem, we'll figure something out."

That caused her to laugh. "Honestly, I'm happy you're having sex."

Toby laughed now too. "I'm happy I'm having sex too."

CHAPTER 27

With her mug of coffee in her hand, Laura stood at the kitchen counter, her eyes closed, and just breathed. She was used to being up early on Saturdays, but on this morning, she wanted to crawl back into bed.

She'd resigned to the fact that she should have gone to Toby's last night, because all she'd done was think about it all night. Oh, she'd seen the dark circles under her eyes when she'd walked past the mirror in the hallway. Thinking about him had cost her precious hours of sleep.

Laura sipped her coffee and then opened her eyes. She had trained her staff to take care of everything. Hadn't she picked the right people and put in the right processes so that every wedding went off without a hitch? And hadn't she done that so she could have an amazing life? And wasn't she supposed to be living that life?

She sipped again.

Well, she wasn't living that life. Driving to Palisade to buy wine, and staying the night, and sleeping with Toby had been the most spontaneous things she'd done in years. And when she'd returned to work, everything had been taken care of. If she didn't show to the wedding, everything would be taken care of.

Laura laughed to herself as she carried her coffee back to her bedroom so she could get ready for the day.

Hours later, Laura stood at the back of the church and watched the bride and groom kiss. She applauded as Irene stepped up to her.

"Everyone is ready for the receiving line. As soon as the bride and groom leave the church for the reception hall after photos, team one will clean up here at the church. Team two is already at the reception venue to make sure everything is in order. I've talked to the bakery, the cake is scheduled for an on time delivery. The florist has also confirmed delivery prior to the reception. I sent Josh up to the picture spot, and he has confirmed that it is ready for photography as soon as they leave here."

Laura turned her head to look at Irene.

"Thank you," she said softly, realizing that she hadn't even asked for any of that information, as she usually would. Irene had simply done the job that Laura trained her to do and had paid her to do.

Irene gave her a quick nod and went on to check another box off the list of things done behind the scenes of a wedding.

Laura looked around. She knew where to look for her team members, and everyone was in place, yet blended into the background. Just as it should be.

She realized she'd watched the entire wedding standing at the back of the church, and hadn't needed to attend to anything.

When Irene walked back by, Laura motioned to her. "Have there been any hiccups?"

Irene shrugged. "Usual. Nothing a safety pin, some tape, or a mint didn't fix," she laughed. "Did someone say anything?"

"No." Laura looked around as the bride and groom began to

make their exit toward them. Stepping out of the way, and taking Irene with her, she watched the wedding party gather in the entry to the church and her team moved in to get everyone in the right places. "I think everything here is running smoothly. I'm going to head out," she said.

Irene's eyes narrowed, but her lips curled into a little smile. "You're going to head out?"

"I've trained you all to take care of this. I have things I need to tend to."

Irene nodded slowly. "We have this. You're right, you trained us, and we can handle this. And I don't mean just this wedding."

Now Laura smiled. Irene had been waiting for years for Laura to loosen up. Perhaps she was finally getting her wish. "I'll see you on Monday then. But you call me if anything, and I mean anything—"

"Goes wrong?" Irene cut her off. "Nothing will go so wrong we can't handle it."

Laura pulled Irene in and hugged her. "Thank you."

"Get," Irene instructed. "And tell the guy who sent you the roses he'd better take care of you."

Laura wanted to argue, but Irene knew her too well.

Toby rubbed his eyes and pushed back from his computer. He needed a hobby that wasn't his work. But he rather enjoyed his work, so it balanced out, didn't it?

As he stood from behind the large oak desk in his home office and stretched, he heard the sound of tires on the gravel. Seriously, if Sarah was coming back for another round of emotional woman talk, he wasn't sure he was ready for it.

Toby walked to the front door and pulled it open. Surely his expression was much different than it had been when Sarah was standing on his front step.

The car in his driveway was Laura's, and when she stepped out of the car in her business suit and her hair pulled back, his heart did a little tumble.

"I didn't expect you," he said, stepping out of the house and walking toward her.

Laura lifted her sunglasses to the top of her head as she moved to him, wrapping her arms around his neck and pressing her body to his so tightly that he had to hold on. Then her mouth came to his and she took him under.

Toby pulled her in tighter, his hand sliding to cup her bottom.

As Laura's tongue tangled with his, her fingers gripped his hair. God, this was better than he could have imagined, he thought.

Toby hoisted her to his hips and turned back to the house.

She hadn't said a word to him yet, and he was damn sure there wasn't going to be any conversations being had. When he reached for the door, she pulled back.

"I missed you," she whispered with her hands cupping his face.

"I missed you, too," he admitted as he fought the door handle.

CHAPTER 28

They lay curled up on the couch in the game room, an old quilt wrapped around them.

Their bodies were slick with sweat, as once again, they'd spent hours worshipping one another. At one point, Laura had told him he was the best sex she'd ever had. At first, the compliment boosted his ego, but now, as they lay together, skin to skin, he wondered what they were doing.

Toby had never been in a real relationship. Not one like his friends had with their significant others. There had always been school or work or building a business. Perhaps Laura's comment meant she was in the same boat. There had never been anything else either.

But he didn't want that anymore.

Shifting, he realized that Laura had fallen asleep. Carefully, he untangled himself from her, maneuvered off the couch, and walked to the bathroom. Opening the small cabinet, he pulled out a pair of shorts and a T-shirt, which he kept in there for when he worked out.

Walking back to the game room, he went behind the bar and pulled a bottle of water out of the refrigerator. As he twisted it open, Laura stirred, then sat up and wrapped the quilt around her.

That smart-looking hairstyle she'd had when she got there, was now a mass of messed hair around her shoulders. The beautifully applied makeup was smeared, and her lips were swollen from hours of kissing. Toby had never seen her look more beautiful.

"When did you get up?" she asked as she walked toward the bar.

"A few minutes ago," he said, offering her the bottle of water. "Are you hungry?"

"What time is it?"

He turned to look at the clock on the wall, which was an illuminated Budweiser sign. "Four."

"We were at it for a long time," she laughed, and then took another sip.

"What happened to your wedding?"

Laura climbed up on the stool. "Oh, I went to the wedding." She reached for his hand. "My team was in control of it. I was just a wallflower. So I left."

Toby smiled. "That's a big deal."

"It is."

"I get it. I need to let my teams do that more too."

Laura tucked a strand of wayward hair behind her ear. "I packed a bag to stay tonight," she admitted, then licked her lips. "Was that your plan?"

Toby nodded. "Yes."

"Tomorrow you play basketball?"

"Yes. I'd love for you to come. I mean, everyone will be coming over afterward for brunch, but you might as well meet them."

Laura pulled back her hand and adjusted the quilt around her. "I'm worried about what Bruce and Sarah will say."

Toby walked around the bar and sat on the stool next to her.

She swiveled so they faced each other. Resting his hands on her knees, he looked into her dark eyes. Wouldn't this tell him where they were headed?

No matter what Sarah said, no matter what happened between him and Laura, it wouldn't ruin any wedding Sarah could have, and it certainly wouldn't mar the marriage she was entering.

However, Toby felt the need to be honest with Laura.

"Sarah knows what's happening between us," he said, and Laura sucked in a breath. "They drive by here. Your car in the driveway all night sends a certain signal."

"Right. I should have expected that."

"Bruce laid it out for me as to when they drove by, and what they observed," he offered. "I can honestly tell you that I didn't kiss and tell, but men don't need that to figure out what's going on."

"I see."

"I have been confronted with it."

Now her eyes went sad. "This is a mistake," Laura said as she moved to hop down from the stool, but Toby kept her in place.

"It's not a mistake. I promised Sarah I wouldn't ruin her wedding."

"She's worried that *you'll* ruin it?"

"She's afraid that if I break your heart…"

Now the sadness in her eyes flashed angry. "What, I'll sabotage her wedding? Why would I do that? Why would I lose everything I've worked for to do that to someone?"

Toby rested his hands on Laura's shoulders and rubbed his thumbs over her skin. "Calm down. Understand where she's coming from. A few months ago she was tied up in a burning shed with some maniac trying to kill her, after he'd killed her best friend. Coming to terms with that, and that your husband will never give you children because he won't pass on his father's genes is a lot to take in. That's why she wants a Laura Torres

135

Wedding with all its sparkle and pizazz. So she's worried that my getting involved with you will rob her of that too."

"Even if this doesn't work out between us, I wouldn't ever…"

"I know that," he quickly confirmed.

Toby eased back and Laura readjusted herself on the stool.

"I'll talk to her," Laura said as she picked up the bottle of water they were now sharing, and took a sip.

"I think she'll appreciate that."

Laura handed him the bottle, and he took a sip.

He watched her now, her mind spinning behind those dark eyes. "Now I have some questions too."

Laura lifted her eyes to meet his. "What kind of questions?"

"About us."

She bit down on her lip. "Okay."

"You said *even if this doesn't work out between us,*" he repeated her words. "What's happening between us?" Her eyes went wide and he knew he needed to amend that quickly. "I mean, I like what's happening between us. I'd like to explore it further."

"Because I jumped into bed with you?"

Toby narrowed his gaze and bit down on the inside of his cheek. "No. Don't think I didn't like that, but what I mean is, I'm interested in more."

"More?"

"Yes. If you're not, I understand. God, how I understand. You and I are so alike when it comes to protecting what we've built, at the expense of relationships and such. But, if this is all just sex, tell me. I'll be okay with it, but then I'll know." He lifted his hand to her cheek and held her gaze. "If you think it could be more, I want to know."

Her lip trembled and he brushed his thumb over it.

"I don't know."

He hadn't expected that, so he nodded, but worked hard to keep his face neutral.

"I've never been in a relationship," she admitted. "I don't know how to make one work."

"Neither do I, but I have a lot of people around me who are making it work."

Laura drew in another breath. "Can we see how it goes? I don't want you to hold it against me if I mess up."

"Isn't that the point? When we mess up, we work it out?"

Laura smiled. "I guess so."

"So, will you be my girlfriend?" he asked and she laughed.

"We're pathetic."

"But I want to be pathetic together."

"So do I." She took his hands and held them in hers. "Before I say yes, I need to ask you to do something for me, and then I'll go with you to the YMCA tomorrow and meet all your friends."

"What do you want me to do?"

She bit down on her lip again. "Let's get dressed. I'm going to take you home to meet my family."

CHAPTER 29

$\mathcal{T}$oby pulled up in front of the house that Laura pointed to.

"Is this where you grew up?" Toby asked.

Laura looked at the house. "No. This would have been a dream, which is why they live here now," she said with pride.

"It's only a few blocks from where Alex and Catherine live."

"More friends?"

"You'll meet them tomorrow. Craig owned the house, but when he got married to Rachel, they moved into her house in Boulder and sold it to Alex when he moved back to Colorado. Bruce lived in their basement."

Laura laughed. "You're all very tight, aren't you?"

"We are. There was a decade we didn't see each other, but I can't imagine not having them all around all the time now."

As he put the car in park and turned off the engine, he noticed Laura staring up at the house.

"Are they expecting us?" Toby asked.

"Not really."

"Not really?"

Laura turned her head toward him. "There is an open door

policy. No, they're not expecting me, but I might show up at any time, and they know that."

"And how many times have you showed up with a *boyfriend*?"

Laura reached for his hand. "I never have."

"I guess we're even. I've never been taken home to someone's family."

"Never?"

"Never."

Laura laughed and it seemed to ease the tension. She looked back at the house. "Things that are certain," she began, "my mother and abuela will be in the kitchen making tamales for lunch tomorrow. My father will be in the living room, in his recliner, watching some Alaska show on Discovery."

"My dad likes those too."

Laura turned back to him. "Maybe let's not tell them we've known each other a week."

"It's nearly been two weeks," he teased. "I'll follow your lead."

Laura nodded and opened her door. Before she could climb from the car, Toby reached for her.

"C'mon, give me an answer. Will you be my girlfriend?" He smiled up at her and she grinned back at him.

"You're childish."

"It's part of my charm."

Laura turned back and leaned over the center console to plant a hard kiss to his lips. "I don't think I have to answer your silly question."

"Oh, but I think you do."

She kissed him hard again.

Toby grinned at her. "Will they be upset that you've only known me a week?"

Her smile softened as she began to climb from the car. "I have to leave some things for you to learn on your own." She winked, stepped out onto the sidewalk, and closed the door.

. . .

Laura waited for Toby to step out of the car and walk around. She took his hand and they walked up the driveway to the back of the house.

When she pulled open the back door, her mother and grand-mother both turned from the counter. They each had on hand-made aprons, and Laura knew she had a matching one on the hook behind the door she'd opened.

"*Mona!*" her grandmother shouted with her hands up in the air, which was Laura's sign to place her face in her grandmother's hands.

She was kissed on both cheeks and then on the lips. When she turned, her mother waited to hug her. Then they both looked toward the door and Laura's stomach tightened.

When she turned, she saw Toby standing at the door, his hands folded in front of him, and a warm grin on his sexy mouth. The welcome she'd received in her parents' home had touched him, she could see it in his eyes. Well, step one, she thought. He hadn't backed out of the door.

"Who did you bring with you?" her mother asked, and Laura noticed her accent was deeper than usual, which happened when her mother was nervous.

Laura held her hand out for Toby, and as he'd said he would, he followed her lead and took her hand.

"*Mamá y Abuelita*, this is Toby Maxwell."

Toby stepped past her and held his hand out to her mother and grandmother.

"It's a pleasure to meet you," he said, and Laura watched both women's eyes go wide with wonder as they shook his hand. "It smells delightful in here," he added and that warranted a wide smile from her grandmother.

"It's nice to meet you too," her mother said.

Laura watched as her grandmother took hold of Toby's face, just as she'd done to Laura. Her grandmother studied him, and then looked in Laura's direction.

"*Es guapo,*" she said, smiling.

Her grandmother let go of his face and continued to talk.

Laura's mother smiled. "She thinks you're handsome, and she wants you to sit down at the table. She's going to get you a tamale."

"Thank you," he said warmly.

Laura grinned as her mother pulled a chair out at the table for him and he sat down.

"I'm going to go say hello to *Papito.*"

Laura touched Toby's shoulder as she passed by him and headed to the living room where her father sat in his recliner, snoring softly.

As Laura neared his chair, his eyes opened, as if he'd sensed her. "Hey, honey," he said, putting the footrest down on his chair and lifting his arms for her to move in and hug him. "I didn't expect you."

"I brought someone home for you to meet," Laura said as she bent over and wrapped her arms around his neck, kissing his cheek before she eased back.

"Someone to meet me?"

"All of you."

Her father's brow rose. "A woman who works for you?"

Laura let out a little laugh. "A man, *Papito.*"

"I don't remember you ever bringing home a man before," he said inching to the edge of his chair.

"I never have."

Standing, her father tucked in his shirt and ran his hands over his hair. "Do I look okay?"

"You look just fine," She said, admiring his silver hair and beard. Laura took her father's arm as they started back toward the kitchen.

CHAPTER 30

*L*esson one in dealing with uncomfortable situations had come Toby's way when he single-handedly made an appointment with the principal in the third grade to discuss the food options in the cafeteria for lunch. He had gathered signatures from kids in kindergarten through the sixth grade on a hand-written petition to get pizza on the menu for Fridays and apple slices as an option instead of squishy peas. Meeting with the principal hadn't been the uncomfortable part, it had been speaking to all of the classes, and back then, sixth graders were scary.

Moving away from home at eighteen and living among teammates who had been lifelong friends had taught Toby how to meld into social groups and belong.

Giving pitches about ideas with hopes of getting venture capitalists interested, that was heart-pumping.

But sitting in the small kitchen with Laura's grandmother and her mother staring at him while he ate a piping hot tamale, that had to have been the most nerve-wracking moment of his life up to that point.

"What do you do for a living, Toby?" her mother asked him as he chewed a hot piece of pork.

He swallowed, feeling the burn in his throat and wishing he had a glass of water. "I own a tech company in Boulder," he explained in the very simplest terms.

"That's quite impressive," she said, and he saw Laura's grandmother nod. It was good to know her grandmother understood English. He wouldn't embarrass himself on purpose then.

"Thank you."

"And how did you meet our Laura?" she continued the interview of him as Laura walked into the kitchen arm in arm with a man that he had to assume was her father.

"*Mamá*, don't hound him," Laura scolded and Toby stood from his seat. "Toby, this is my *Papito.*"

Toby held out his hand to the man, who first looked him over, exchanged a look with both Laura's mother and grandmother, then with Laura, before shaking Toby's hand.

"It's nice to meet you," her father said with a firm grip of Toby's hand.

"Toby is originally from Texas, played college basketball, and owns a tech company in Boulder," Laura informed her father as he continued to shake Toby's hand.

"You don't say? What position did you play?" her father asked.

"Point guard, sir."

Her father nodded and finally let go of Toby's hand. "What do you think of the Nuggets this year?"

"I think they have a chance, but I honestly don't follow them as much as I do college ball."

"C.U.?"

"Of course. But I find collegiate still has some heart."

Her father's eyes softened. "Couldn't agree more."

∾

As had been the norm Laura's entire life, no visit was less than three hours long, was filled with food, and at least one, if not more, relatives showing up to visit as well.

By the time she was able to make her way out of her parents' house, she was exhausted.

Nearing Toby's house, Laura turned to him, realizing they hadn't spoken the entire drive home.

"Thank you," she said softly, and he reached for her hand.

"You don't have to thank me."

"I feel as if I do. That had to be more than you bargained for. My parents, my grandmother, my auntie, three cousins, and a nosy neighbor."

Toby chuckled. "That's what meeting the family is all about, right?"

"If we'd been together more than a week, I could have talked you up which would have squelched some of the questions."

"Well we can't fix our time frame."

"They didn't scare you away? I mean we haven't said a word to each other since we left. I'm overwhelmed. How can you not be?"

Toby turned down the road that would lead to his house. "I deal with inquisition and details every day of my life. Your family is protective of you. I can't just be some guy you're sleeping with. That won't work for your family."

Laura pulled her hand back from his and wrung her hands together. "I didn't tell them that part."

"Tell me that part," he said as he pulled up in front of the house and pushed the button to open the garage door. "Tell me that there's more between us than just that."

"I thought we already agreed on that."

"You never answered my question."

"What question?"

Toby pulled the car into the garage, turned off the engine, and pushed the button to close the garage door. "The one about being my girlfriend."

"You seriously want an answer to that?"

"I could put it on a note and ask you to check a box," he teased, but Laura wasn't sure where the conversation was really going.

"You're teasing. So they didn't scare you?"

The light in the garage turned off and they still sat in the car, now in the dark. "I've had to convince people to give me millions of dollars on just an idea and then work my ass off not to lose those millions of dollars. That scares me. Loving a woman with a family who cares about her, I can walk that line. I'm not going to hurt you. I'm going to learn about you. I'm going—"

"Back it up," she interrupted him. "You said *loving a woman.*"

"I did."

"What does that mean?"

Toby narrowed his gaze on her. "What do you think it means?"

"Are you going to keep turning questions back?"

"Take it how you want. I want more than what we've been doing. I have to assume you do too because you took me to meet your family." He opened the door and the dome light had Laura wincing from the brightness. "I'm good with partnerships, Laura. Even partnerships that start with a limited relationship," he said as he stepped out of the car.

Laura gathered her things, including the bag of tamales her grandmother had sent with her. She opened the door to the car and stepped out into the garage. The light turned on by their motion, and they both stood looking at each other over the top of the car.

"My mother is going to want more information," she said, and it echoed through the garage.

"What kind of information is she going to want?"

"She's going to want to know our intentions. This is why I've never taken a man home."

"Then figure out your intentions," he said as he walked toward the door, punched in a code, and let himself into the house.

Laura stood there and the light turned off again, leaving her in the dark. Was he telling her he loved her? Was that what he wanted when he said he wanted more? Was that what she wanted? God, she was used to having sex with men, but not having to think about more than that. That wasn't how she wanted it to be forever, and she knew that. But she needed to decide how much she was willing to give in her life just to have access to Toby's house, because wasn't that why she was there?

The thought that perhaps that's why she was there at all squeezed at her heart.

Did she think she loved him? She did take him home, she considered. But what if she didn't really know, and she was using him in the only way she knew?

Now her heart ached in her chest and she wasn't sure what to think about it all.

CHAPTER 31

When Laura forced her eyes open on Sunday morning, they stung. Oh, the rest of the evening hadn't gone as she'd have liked. Between Toby's garage and his house, she'd fallen apart.

It was her own doing to leave and spend the night in her own bed. And even after she'd made a fool of herself in a crying fit over not knowing where she wanted to take this new and strange relationship, Toby had called to make sure she'd made it home okay.

Laura wiped her eyes and realized she'd never even taken off her makeup, when her fingers were smeared with black eyeliner and mascara. She was surprised there'd been any makeup left after all the tears.

Pushing back the sheets, she shifted her feet to the floor and slipped them into her slippers. She sat on the edge of the bed for a moment to collect herself.

When she felt as if she could walk through the dimly lit house, she headed to the kitchen to make herself a cup of coffee.

The light on the microwave said it was five o'clock, and Laura hated that even on a Sunday she couldn't sleep in. And today, she'd really like to just sleep all day.

Setting her *Sunday* mug under the drip on the coffee machine, she added a pod, and pressed the button. As the machine whirred to life, Laura leaned against the counter. Toby had basketball that morning with his friends and brunch after. Nowhere in her fit-throwing did he ask her not to come.

But was it a good idea to even consider going? Perhaps she should figure out her intentions, as she said they needed to do, before she saw him again.

When the coffee finished brewing, she took the mug and held it between her hands. Through the blinds in her kitchen, she could see the slightest sliver of light on the horizon. Her grandmother would say that was God giving her another day to cherish everything she had, and everyone. Her mother would say that daylight brought opportunity to change the world. A smile formed on her lips. Pride swelled in her chest at the thought of what her parents did every day to make sure Laura had the education and opportunities to become who she had—a successful businesswoman.

Sipping her coffee, Laura thought about the first wedding she'd planned. Her Aunt Juanita had met a man named George and they fell in love.

George's family wasn't thrilled that he was marrying a bilingual woman whose citizenship was as new as a shiny penny. They cut him off from everything for going through with his marriage to Juanita.

Laura hated the idea that someone would push away their child for loving someone who spoke a different language and whose skin was darker than theirs. Perhaps that was why her parents had always been critical of who Laura dated, they didn't want someone to hate her enough to push away their own child if she loved them.

She set the coffee mug on the counter and pressed her fingers to her eyes.

Perhaps that was why Laura had never let a relationship get past sex, and why she'd never taken a man home.

Her hands began to shake when she realized that her mother and grandmother had managed to get Toby at a table and Laura had walked out to get her father. In that time, had they freaked him out? Had he felt as if he'd been in front of a firing squad?

No, he would have said something, right?

Then Juanita showed up, and even a woman who married a light-skinned man and went through the scrutiny of his family hating her, had her own questions.

God, Laura should have listened when Toby answered their inquisitions.

She thought back to the hours around the kitchen table with tamales. Half of the conversations weren't even in English, but Toby hadn't seemed to mind. He didn't ask if they were talking behind his back, or even question what the conversation was.

She hadn't even noticed that her own conversations with her family had slipped in and out of English and Spanish.

And yet he'd still wanted more from her—relationship wise. He wanted her to commit to being his girlfriend.

Laughter snuck through the tears that threatened.

He'd asked her to be his girlfriend.

Laura laughed harder now. Having been part of hundreds of wedding vows, she'd never considered the simplicity with which each couple decided that they were actually a couple.

Toby Maxwell was simple—and she was making the entire situation complicated.

Laura blew out a breath, picked up her coffee mug, and took a sip.

Perhaps it was her own fear of rejection that had kept her from ever loving a man. Her business was built around lavish weddings where couples professed their love for one another for the rest of their lives—but nearly half of those marriages ended in divorce. Though that had never bothered her, or she'd never given it much thought, now she wondered if long term scared her.

Toby had partnerships with companies worth millions of dollars. Partnerships were long term.

Laura had contracts for events that happened and then they were over.

Her heart raced when she realized she didn't understand commitment.

Sipping her coffee again, she wondered when she'd lost the part of herself that wanted that kind of happiness. Her parents had it, even though they worked harder than any other people she'd ever met, they were committed to one another and their family. Her grandparents had been committed to one another. Even George had stuck around until a heart attack stole him from Juanita.

Her family had worked hard and shared their wealth—not financial wealth, but the wealth of love. Laura realized that she'd missed out on the meaning of it all. Working hard, having a fancy car, owning her own house and business had netted her a lot of glory and money, but she'd forgotten to let in the one aspect that made it all work—love.

Turning, Laura poured the still steaming coffee down the drain. She had a basketball game to attend and a brunch after.

And she needed to let Toby know she was ready to be his girlfriend.

CHAPTER 32

*a*n empty basketball court still could calm Toby's nerves.

He'd arrived at the YMCA nearly an hour earlier than game time just to have some time to clear his mind. Free throws, layups, three pointers—each one of them went through the basket.

When Bruce caught the ball under the net, Toby realized his alone time was up.

"I haven't seen you alone on the court for a long time, my friend," Bruce called out as he dribbled the ball from hand to hand. "What's on your mind?"

Only someone Toby considered a brother would know his tells.

"Women," he said. "A woman," he corrected.

Bruce took the ball and carried it to center court where he looked Toby in the eye. "I'll lose my shit if you did something to that woman that is going to upset Sarah."

The statement should have angered Toby, but he found an endearing quality in Bruce's need to give Sarah everything she wanted—especially the fancy wedding.

"I didn't do anything to her. She took me home to meet her

family and that seemed to upset her. That or me asking her to be my girlfriend."

Bruce blinked hard. "You've known her a week and half and you asked her to be your girlfriend? What are you, ten?"

Toby chuckled and pulled the ball from Bruce's hands and sunk the ball from center court. When it bounced, Alex caught it in one hand and held Celia Rose in the other arm.

"You still have mad skill, my friend," he said as he bounced the ball back to Toby.

Bruce's eyes were narrowed on Toby. "Seriously, man, don't mess this up for Sarah."

"If I thought that's what I was doing, I'd stop."

"Then what are you doing?" Bruce asked as Catherine and Rachel walked through the door followed by Sarah and then Craig who carried a sleeping baby on his shoulder.

"I'm falling in love."

The coffee in Laura's hand had probably been a mistake. Her stomach tightened and her knees wobbled as she walked through the front door of the YMCA.

His game should have started twenty minutes ago. Laura was walking into a lion's den, she thought. All eyes would be on her.

She was used to that, somewhat. Head up, shoulders back, smile locked in place, and ignore the butterflies that threaten to make her sick, she reminded herself.

Following the sounds of sneakers on hardwood, Laura found the gym and stood in the hallway for a moment. Bruce had jumped and the ball went through the net. He called out some claim that he was a god, and then stopped when he saw her.

"Hey," he called and Laura lifted a hand as if she couldn't find her voice.

Bruce walked toward her. "Did you come to watch me take Toby down?"

"Oh, that's quite competitive," she laughed.

"Every week. Someone usually walks out of here with a black eye, jammed finger, or a twisted ankle."

"Perhaps there shouldn't be a game before your wedding," she teased and noticed that Toby was slowly walking toward them.

"Don't let this guy make you think he's all that," Toby said, his eyes locked on hers.

"I guess I'll have to watch and make my own judgements," she confirmed.

Bruce shifted a glance between them before wrapping his arm around Laura's shoulders and escorting her across the court.

"Toby doesn't know how to be social, so let me help him." They stopped mid court. "This is Alex, Craig, and Ray," he said the names and each man shook her hand. "You know Sarah," he said and Sarah moved in to hug her.

"It's nice to see you," Sarah said, but Laura felt the bite in it as if she wasn't actually happy that she was there.

In time, Laura thought. She understood the nerves.

Bruce continued to walk her toward the small set of bleachers where three other women sat with young kids and babies.

"This is our fan club," he laughed and one of the women stood.

"Leave her alone. We can take it from here," the woman whose arm was completely tattooed with an ocean scene with a baby on her hip said. "I'm Rachel and this is Angela. I'm Craig's wife."

"It's nice to meet you," Laura said.

Rachel turned to the others. "This is Catherine, Celia Rose, and Gretchen," she pointed to the baby in Catherine's arms. "They are Alex's family."

"Hello," Laura offered.

"And Kelly, Connor, and Charlotte are Ray's family."

"It's nice to meet you all," Laura said as Charlotte walked up to her, a teddy bear in her arms, and looked up at her.

"I'm five now," she said.

Laura knelt down so she was eye to eye with the little girl. "You are? That's a big number." Laura tapped the nose of the bear that Charlotte carried. "And who is this?"

Charlotte turned the bear around as if to show it to Laura. "This is Cuddles. We keep him to remind us of our baby in heaven with Grandpa," she said, and Laura had to ward off the instant tears.

"What an important bear," Laura acknowledged.

"You can sit with us. This is where the mommies sit." Charlotte moved back to sit next to her brother and play on the iPad he instantly shared with her.

Kelly shook her head as Laura stood. "She's not shy," she said.

"I was much like that when I was little too, and I carried a ratty old bear for the very same reason."

Connor looked up when Laura said that. "You had a baby go to heaven too?"

Laura nodded. "Two of them, actually. I never got to meet them."

"We didn't meet our baby either," he confirmed and then looked back down at the iPad.

Kelly patted the bench next to her. "And now you know more about our family than you could have imagined. Tell us about you."

Laura sat down and held her coffee between her hands. She shifted a glance, and a smile, between each of the women. "I'm Sarah's wedding planner."

Catherine nodded. "She's very excited to work with you."

"That makes me happy. I appreciate when my work speaks for itself. She's going to have a very nice wedding."

Rachel adjusted the baby in her arms. "She deserves it too. They both do."

Laura looked out at the court and caught Toby's eye. He smiled sweetly as Sarah plowed her shoulder into him to catch the ball intended for him. He laughed when Sarah shot it and scored, then he looked at Laura again.

Charlotte stood again and walked to Laura. "Why are you here?"

Laura had forgotten that little kids could be so forward.

"I'm here to watch them play basketball."

"Why?" she asked again.

"Because I'm Toby's girlfriend," she confirmed and then looked up to see that he had heard her commit to him.

CHAPTER 33

*a*s the families gathered up their belongings, the volume in the gym grew louder than when they were playing.

The men who had been chirping at each other for the past two hours now complimented one another on plays they had made. Toby and Bruce were talking about work. Craig mentioned something about giving a test to his students, and Alex and Ray both scoffed at that.

The women who had surrounded Laura scurried to put bags back together of items that had been used while they'd sat together and taken care of their families. They discussed nachos and margaritas, and Sarah picked up Celia Rose and bounced her around on her hip as the little girl squealed.

Laura couldn't help but think that her loud family had nothing on this group. Perhaps that was why Toby hadn't been nervous to meet her family. His family, those he spent time with and cherished, were just as overwhelming as her own.

Ray slapped a hand on Toby's shoulder as he picked up his daughter. "We'll see you in an hour. Charlotte made some cookies and a poster for this morning," he said and Charlotte nodded.

"I get to tell you something," she said before Ray covered her mouth with his hand and she giggled.

Toby moved in next to Laura and wrapped his arm around her waist. "Like a secret?" he asked Charlotte.

Charlotte nodded with her father's hand still covering her mouth.

"Kids, huh?" Ray laughed as he and his family walked out of the gym.

Each of them had similar goodbyes, and soon, it was only Toby and Laura standing in the gym.

He took her hands, kissed her fingers, then wrapped her arms around him. She laughed as he still held her hands, now behind his back.

"The wives of your friends are charming," Laura complimented.

"They are."

"Rachel's tattoo is amazing."

Toby nodded. "It is."

"What are the scars on her shoulder?"

Toby began to sway as if he heard music she couldn't. "She was shot."

Laura jerked against him as she stopped swaying. Her mouth had fallen open, and she quickly closed it. "Shot? As in someone with a gun shot her?"

Toby nodded and made her body sway again. "The tattoo on her arm covers scars from cutting and a suicide attempt," he said, his voice soft and calm.

Laura felt no calm in that. "That's horrible."

"It led to her life's work. She's a therapist. She lost her brother to suicide, took a dark turn, and now she's very mindful of mental health and helping people. She's been immensely helpful getting me through the situation with Sarah and Bruce."

"Did the man that abducted Sarah shoot Rachel?"

Toby shook his head. "No. She was caught in the crossfire of a school shooting when she was trying to help a boy who needed her."

Laura stopped again. "I remember that."

"Hard to forget," Toby agreed and leaned in to press a kiss to her lips.

"Catherine's daughters are very close in age," Laura continued with her observations.

"Celia Rose is Alex's. Her mother died in a car accident and Catherine adopted her. Then they had Gretchen."

"I take back the charming comment."

Toby stopped swaying and moved so that their hands were no longer behind him, but between them.

"You don't think they're charming?" She could hear the offense in his voice.

"I think they're miraculous."

The smile on his lips returned. "I could go with that." He stepped in closer to her, their hands still connected. "You told Charlotte you were my girlfriend."

"I did," she admitted.

"That made me very happy."

"I gave it a lot of thought this morning. I want to be your girlfriend."

Toby leaned in and kissed her again gently. "Someday it won't have only been a week and a half that we've known each other. Someday it'll be months, years, and a lifetime."

Her heart hammered in her chest. "That's a lot to think about."

"I think about it."

"Let's get through brunch first, and then maybe I can wrap my head around another week."

Toby nodded, but he didn't let her go. "You also told Charlotte you carried a bear for the same reason she does."

"I did."

"These are all those things I look forward to learning. Tell me about it."

Laura looked around the empty gym. "Now?"

"Right now."

She swallowed hard. "My mother lost a set of twins when I was six. They were five months into her pregnancy. She had to have a C-section and we had a huge funeral for them." Laura bit down on her lip to keep her teeth from chattering recalling the trauma her mother went through. "I carried that bear until I was ten to remind me of my sisters."

"Where is that bear now?"

The thought made her smile. "On my bed."

"I love that family is that important to you."

"It is."

He nodded. "Kelly and Ray lost their baby at the first of the year. They had just gotten back together."

"They were apart?"

"Divorced for two years."

She found that tears were frequent when she was around Toby. Usually she wasn't so emotional, but she could be around him.

"And they're together again?"

"Their wedding night was the night that Bruce and Sarah finally got together."

"You're surrounded by love," Laura said as Toby pulled her in closer and wrapped his arms around her.

"I am. That's why I believe in it so much."

"But you've never been in love?"

"Never."

"I'm scared to death."

Toby pressed a kiss to her forehead. "So am I. But what partnership doesn't have a bit of fear?"

"I suppose."

Toby released her, picked up his gym bag, and then took her hand. "Let's get home. I want to get a bottle of champagne out and some sparkling cider for the kids."

"Why?" Laura laughed as they walked out of the gym. "I have a feeling Charlotte's secret warrants it."

CHAPTER 34

oby had been right. Everyone had convened into his kitchen with the dishes they had brought for brunch when Charlotte and Connor marched into the room with their homemade sign that read, WE'RE HAVING A BABY!

The women around Laura screamed as they rushed Kelly and wrapped her in their arms.

"I can't believe it," Catherine shouted above all the voices. "I always know when someone is pregnant. Why didn't I know you were pregnant?"

Kelly shrugged. "You're losing your touch."

Rachel hugged Kelly hard and then eased back. "You're okay? Everything is okay? The baby is good?"

Kelly took Ray's hand. "We're far enough along that they've confirmed that the baby is right where she's supposed to be. For now," Kelly said with caution, "everything seems to be just right."

Ray kissed his wife's head. "She's a champ, this one." He rested his hand on his wife's belly. "So is she," he said, referring to the baby.

"A girl," Rachel clasped her hands together. "Another girl?"

Kelly nodded. "Connor is going to need someone to have some boys."

They all laughed, but Laura felt those damned tears in her throat and she swallowed them down.

Toby popped the cork on the champagne and all heads turned. "I kind of thought this was going to be a morning for celebration. But Charlotte kept her secret."

He poured glasses of champagne and sparkling cider. Covered dishes were uncovered, plates were filled, and noise filled the house.

Laura felt right at home.

With a full plate, Laura carried her meal to the table in the dining room and sat down. As she crossed her legs and placed her napkin on her lap, Sarah walked into the room and sat down next to her.

It was only then did Laura feel uncomfortable. How was she supposed to handle herself around Sarah in this situation? Was there an on and off switch for professionalism and friendship? Laura had no idea, she'd never fallen into this predicament before.

"It was nice that you came to the game this morning," Sarah said as she arranged her plate and placed her napkin in her lap.

"It was fun. You're very good," she complimented Sarah's athletic skills.

"Yeah, full rides for me too," she boasted. "And Alex thought he was using me for practice. Look who got the goods."

"It must have been fun to grow up around all of these guys."

Sarah shrugged. "I wasn't around most of them. Just Alex and Bruce. By the time they were in college, I was just breaking out in zits." Sarah loaded up her fork with macaroni salad and ate it. "I've gotten to know the rest of them the past few years after their coach died. Well, after Rachel's dad died."

"It seems as if he brought them all back together again."

"That's true enough." Sarah lifted a slice of cucumber to her mouth then lowered it. "I have to admit something to you. I wasn't sure how I was going to react around you socially," she said, and Laura felt the twisting in her stomach tighten.

"Why is that?"

"I mean, I hired you for a job. I got Toby involved in something he didn't want to do. And now," she drew out the word. "Now you're dating?"

Laura lifted her napkin to her lips and wiped them before realizing she hadn't even eaten anything. But it gave her a moment of pause.

"We are."

"You just met."

"We did. And talk about a rocky start, huh? He went from ordering me off his property to wanting me around."

Sarah dragged her fork through something that looked like a gelatin salad before lifting her eyes back to Laura. "I'd understand if you don't want to work with me anymore. I don't want to get in the way of Toby finding happiness."

Laura leaned in and rested her hand on Sarah's arm. "Why wouldn't I want to work with you? I'm very excited to be part of your wedding."

"I just don't want Toby to get hurt. I mean you were after getting to use the house. I got you into the house."

Laura eased back, and she knew where that fine line was now. This had to be all professional or she was on the verge of Sarah walking out on her.

"It might have started that way, but I feel as if I have a greater vested interest now. I care very deeply for Toby, and I know that's important to you, as much as your own wedding."

"It is."

"And though I would have done nearly anything to use the

house for a venue, I wouldn't use him," she promised Sarah, and herself.

Sarah nodded and eased back in her chair. "I'm sorry. I sound as if I'm accusing you of doing something wrong." She pushed away her plate. "The closer we get to the wedding, I find myself freaking out. I know for the next month I'll be working very closely with you on little details. I mean, hell, it's only been a week, right?"

Laura forced the smile on her lips to stay put as she nodded.

Sarah leaned in, bracing her elbows on the table. "Rachel and my therapist tell me that I'll go through this a lot. Having attention showered on me will trigger negative feelings after my attack."

Laura felt the control to keep the smile slip, but she kept her attention on Sarah.

Sarah set her napkin on the table. "It's silly, right?"

Laura shook her head. "No. What you went through is very serious. Sarah, if I can help you in any way with your recovery, please let me know. I don't want this to be harmful to you, but I want to give you the wedding of your dreams. The wedding you deserve."

As Sarah readjusted herself in her chair again, her eyes were lighter, as if Laura might have saved the moment.

"I appreciate that. Just know that when I get like this, it's not personal. I mean, it's not personal if you really care for Toby and aren't using him."

"I promise."

"And I'm going to freak out a lot more. I know this."

"I'll make sure to work with that. You're not the first bride to have her mind in all different places," Laura said, knowing full well Sarah was the first bride Laura had worked with who had been through something so traumatic publicly. "I will do everything in my power to make your day is memorable, special, and yours."

"Thank you," she said as Alex called for Sarah and she stood. "I'm looking forward to coming to your place next week to pick out the detail pieces."

The smile was natural now as Laura looked up at her. "It's one of my favorite parts of wedding planning."

Sarah turned to find her brother, leaving her plate on the table. She paused and looked back at Laura. "Toby's an amazing man."

"I think so too."

CHAPTER 35

To appease her mother, Laura had spent the past two nights at her parents' house for dinner. Though she would have like to have had Toby there with her, so that she wasn't asked the million and one questions she had been, she understood that sometimes his work took him away without notice.

And hadn't that warranted her mother's concern? What did a man do when he up and left like that? Laura thought the question had been absurd, but it was how her mother thought.

As Laura set up the design room on Wednesday morning for Sarah's design meeting, her phone rang. She pulled it from the pocket of her suit, looked at the ID, and smiled.

"Good morning, handsome," she said, closing the door to the room.

"Hey, beautiful," Toby's voice said. "I miss you."

"I miss you too. How is L.A.?"

"Ugly. It's not my favorite city, but there is a lot of money just floating around out here. Tech is hot and I'm their guy."

Laura fanned out the napkin samples in front of her. "And what does Bruce think of it?"

That had Toby chuckling. "He's never been anywhere, so he's like a tourist. It's kind of embarrassing." She heard Bruce's protest in the background.

"How much longer will you be out there?"

"A few more days."

"I'm not sure I can handle that," she chuckled. "My mother has had me over each night so she can quiz me about you. I'm running out of information."

"You could fly out here and be with me," he offered.

Laura laughed. "No I can't. I have an enormous wedding on Saturday, and the rehearsal dinner on Friday."

Toby sighed. "So even when I get home we won't have any time together?"

"It sounds like it. I could hire you to be a server," she teased but he didn't say anything right away. "Or you could do set up and clean up."

"If it means I could be with you, I'd do it."

"I was kidding."

"I'm not," his voice was somber.

The intercom buzzed in the corner of the room. "Miss Burke is here," Irene said through the speaker.

"I have to go," Laura said into the phone.

"We'll be home soon. Bruce says to make sure Sarah picks out anything she wants."

"I'll make sure of it."

They said their goodbyes and Laura walked out to the lobby where Sarah, Rachel, and Catherine all stood looking at the photos of weddings that graced the walls.

"Hi, ladies," she said and all three heads turned toward her.

Rachel pointed to the photo they'd been looking at. "You planned Courtney Jensen's wedding?"

Laura looked at the photo of the Olympic skier atop the snow-covered mountain in her custom-made wedding dress and a beautiful Colorado sunset behind her.

"I did. It's one of the only weddings I've planned that we supplied oxygen."

Sarah hiked her purse up on her shoulder. "I hope it's okay I brought them with me. Since Bruce isn't here, I thought they could help me with everything."

"Of course it's okay. Before we go back, can I offer you all anything to drink? Wine, champagne, soda, water?"

"I'll take a glass of champagne," Sarah said.

"I can make it a mimosa since it's early."

"Let's do it."

Laura looked at the other two who wrinkled up their noses.

"I'll take a water," Rachel sighed. "Still breastfeeding."

"Me too," Catherine said.

Laura smiled. "Let me show you where we'll be, and I'll have Irene bring in your drinks."

As they passed Irene's desk, Laura gave her the drink orders, and escorted Toby's friends to the design room.

"Wow," Sarah said as she looked around the room.

Laura closed the glass door behind them. "That's your board," she pointed to the one on the wall which was not covered with a piece of satin and a bow. "We build each wedding visually."

"And the ones covered up?"

Laura smiled. "Each wedding is kept private."

Sarah's eyes softened, and Laura thought she was grateful for that detail.

"These are nice pictures of Toby's house."

Laura let out a sigh. "They should be. They almost got me arrested."

All three women looked back at her.

"I don't think he actually would have had you arrested," Rachel said.

"I'm not so sure."

"Well, he certainly wouldn't now. The man is head over heels in love with you," she said as she turned and looked back at the board.

Laura clasped her hands together because they shook now. "I don't know about that." She swallowed hard. "Why don't we get started," she suggested and heard her voice shake.

For the next two hours, Sarah sipped on her mimosas and picked out linens, invitations, bouquets, and all the little details that would make her big day shine. Rachel and Catherine drank glasses of water with lemon from crystal glasses, and they all ate through the plates of cookies that Irene supplied and resupplied.

"If you have time next week, or the week after, we can arrange a cake tasting."

The eyes of all three women grew wide.

Sarah leaned in on her elbows. "Bruce will love that, but can I bring them too?" She nodded toward Rachel and Catherine.

"Of course. In fact, if you're interested, I could arrange it so that we do a tasting with everyone."

"I would love that."

"We'll make that happen," Laura jotted down the note on her legal pad. "I also wanted to ask, since your wedding is the day after Christmas, do you want holiday decor still up? Or would you like it taken down?"

Sarah chewed her lip as she considered. "I hadn't thought about that, but I think I'd like to have it up. I mean, I'll still be celebrating."

Laura made note of that as well.

"Well, that's everything for now. I'll get your invitations ordered, and if you'll get me your guest list and addresses, we'll send them out to calligraphy as soon as they arrive so that we can get them mailed in time. We'll also send out save-the-date cards."

Sarah smiled wide. "I can't believe this is all in motion. Then again, I still can't believe I'm marrying Bruce."

Catherine laughed. "Neither can your brother," she said, referencing her husband. "He's happy for you, now, but he still can't believe after all of these years of forbidding anything between the two of you, now you're at this point."

"And I'm happier than I've ever been," Sarah finished her mimosa. "I mean, deliriously happy. Okay, some of that might be because my brother forbade it."

They all laughed as they stood from the table. Rachel reached her hand to Laura's arm. "Why don't you join us tomorrow night for nachos and margaritas?"

"Oh, that sounds fun."

"We do it every week. The guys usually end up at Toby's," she added. "And, there will be a day when we can actually have margaritas again. I mean, well, most of us. You and Sarah can enjoy as many as you'd like."

"I'll be there."

When they'd left, Laura returned to her office and closed the door. There was a lightness in her heart. She couldn't remember the last time she'd been invited out to a girls' night. Weddings had been her entire life for years. She couldn't have imagined that in the course of securing a venue she dreamed of and planning another wedding, that she'd make new friends—and fall in love.

CHAPTER 36

*L*aura pulled up to the restaurant where Toby's friends had told her to meet them for nachos and margaritas. She pulled down her visor and inspected herself in the mirror.

Having left work late, she was still dressed in her suit, but her top wasn't see-through, so going into the restaurant wasn't going to stir anyone up as it had when she'd stopped by Toby's two weeks ago.

Taking her lipstick out of her purse, Laura ran the color over her lips and thought about the fateful night she'd gone to Toby's to have him sign the contract that had been missing. Surely it wasn't the top she'd worn that had changed her life that day. The thought had her laughing to herself as she capped her lipstick and slid it back into her purse.

Stepping out of her car, she smelled a familiar scent. A moment later she realized it was Toby's cologne.

"Hello, beautiful," his voice came from behind her and she spun to see him standing at the back of her car.

Laura moved to him swiftly, wrapping her arms around his neck, nearly knocking him over as she pressed her lips to his.

"I didn't know you were coming home today," she said between kisses.

"We didn't either." He pressed his forehead to hers. "So you got invited to nachos and margaritas. You're in the circle now."

"Is that what this means?"

"Yes. I guess you're stuck with me now." He let his hands slip over her bottom as he swayed them right there in the parking lot as if they were the only people around.

"I don't think that would be a horrible thing," she admitted.

"I'm glad to hear you say that." Toby pressed a kiss to her forehead. "Bruce ran in to see Sarah. We're going to head over to Alex's for guys' night."

"I've heard this is how Thursdays go."

"And now you're in the fold," he kissed her lips softly. "Spend the night with me when you're done."

"Fridays are very busy for me," she sighed. "I don't know."

"I could spend the night with you if that helps."

Laura laughed. "I'm not sure that would change anything. You've only been gone a few days, and I missed you—a lot."

Toby let out a low hum, which was nearly a growl. "Then let's get home early," he offered as he pulled Laura closer and she knew their needs were the same.

"I'll meet you at your house," she said on an airy sigh.

"I'll text you the code to the garage."

"People are watching," Bruce's voice interrupted their interlude.

Laura eased back from Toby, but now she was rethinking going inside. He had a way of stirring her up and making her mind go completely blank.

"I'm glad you're both home," Laura said in response to Bruce's remark as she let her hand slide into Toby's.

"He was missing you so much, he cancelled his last meeting," Bruce said. "That's a big deal."

Laura looked up at Toby who grinned and then shrugged.

"You know the saying about meetings that could be emails?" He and Bruce laughed, but Laura couldn't help but wonder if she were getting in the way of his business. She knew she certainly wasn't as focused as she'd have liked to have been.

Toby pulled her to him again and planted a kiss to her lips that had the evening's heat sizzling up her spine.

"I'll see you at home," he said as he pulled back.

With her mind scrambled, Laura only nodded. Then he stepped from her and Bruce moved in to kiss her on the cheek before both men walked through the parking lot and to Toby's car a few rows away.

Laura took a few more moments to collect herself before she walked into the restaurant to find the women who had invited her into their circle.

Rachel waved from a table in the corner. Seated next to her, in a high chair, was Angela, who was seated next Charlotte, and Celia Rose. Catherine nursed Gretchen at the table and had lifted her head from a conversation with Kelly to watch Laura walk toward the table. It was then she realized that Sarah was the missing person.

"She ran to the bathroom," Rachel said, obviously understanding Laura's confusion. "It appears that she's become a sap now that's she's fallen in love. Bruce surprised her and she cried."

"Understandable. I see it happen to brides all the time," Laura admitted as she took the unoccupied seat next to Rachel and sat down.

"I'm glad you joined us. I assume Toby found you?"

Laura felt her cheeks heat. "He did."

"I have known the man most of my life. I have to tell you, I've never seen him as happy as he is now."

"Really?"

Rachel nodded. "He was the quiet one. The studious one. The caretaker."

Laura smiled. "I could see that."

Sarah returned from the bathroom and smiled at Sarah. "I'm glad they're home safe," she said as she sat down in the empty chair. "Bruce gets anxious when he travels. He's always afraid his past will find him in different places, like someone will know him from back then."

Laura wondered how someone could live like that, always looking over their shoulder.

Sarah poured herself a drink from the pitcher of margarita and held it to offer one to Laura.

"I think I will," Laura said taking the empty glass in front of her and pushing it toward Sarah.

"I told Bruce about the cake tasting. He can't wait."

Laura smiled. "I think it'll be more fun with everyone."

"Mommy says I get to come too," Charlotte said holding each of the toddlers' hands to her sides. "I like cake."

"Then you're really going to have a good time," Laura promised as she lifted her margarita to her lips.

Looking around the table at the women who had invited her into their circle, she thought about the stories she'd heard of each of them.

Rachel's tattoo hid secrets to who she'd become and the traumas she'd endured.

Catherine was raising the daughter of her husband and a stranger who had died.

Kelly was pregnant with her rainbow baby, and her daughter shared her special bear with the toddlers on either side of her.

Sarah was marrying a man she'd always loved and had been forbidden to be with—well, Laura wondered how serious that was. Then again, now knowing Bruce's background, she understood it.

The man that brought her to this table was still a stranger to her. These women had known the men they loved most of their lives.

She'd never considered forever and happily ever after for herself. Oh, she sold it every single day of her life. It paid for her house, her car, and her suits. But why hadn't she thought it was for her?

And was her happily ever after with Toby? She'd read enough romance novels with quick love, then again, those were characters in a book and she would never find out if it was forever or for the moment.

But was forever what she and Toby had, or was it just sex?

She sipped the margarita, but it was sour on her tongue. No, sex had never stirred her up like being with Toby did. Sex never set her at a table with amazing women either.

Patience was never one of Laura's greater virtues. Could she be patient enough to find out if what she'd felt for the past few weeks was real? Once Sarah's wedding was over, would she be forgotten by them all—including Toby?

Laura sipped her drink again. The women around her laughed and chatted, and somehow that had thrown her into her own pity party.

CHAPTER 37

It was nine o'clock when Laura looked down at her phone for the code that Toby had texted her. There was a four digit code to punch in so she could park in the garage, another code to get into the door through the garage, and yet one more to turn off the alarm.

Laura's phone shook in her hand when she realized he'd nearly handed over everything to her with one text.

It took her nearly ten minutes to go through each step because her nerves made her sick. As she silenced the alarm and stood in the mudroom, in the silent and dark house she'd admired, she sucked in a breath and tried to will the hammering of her heart to ease.

Toby wouldn't have given her the codes to come and go as freely as she liked if he didn't trust her. After all, wasn't he in the middle of his own mental health crisis over trust?

Laura set her purse on the bench in the mudroom and then leaned herself up against the dryer, just to take a moment. What did it really mean that she was in his house alone—and not expected to clean it?

She'd known the man three weeks, and in those three weeks

they'd had more of a relationship than she'd had with men she dated for months or years. Okay, she'd never dated a man for years. What was wrong with her?

She and Toby had started in an argument, and worked toward like over a game of pool. There was the impromptu dinner invite that led to a business trip. And, damn, hadn't that trip changed everything? She learned secrets that were kept, fears that were had, and she watched the man in his own element—business element. He'd taken care of her, and then they'd fallen into bed.

Maybe things were supposed to go faster in your thirties, she considered. When she thought about the fact that she'd already introduced him to her family, which she'd been fielding questions about for those three weeks, and he'd introduced her to his friends, that should have taken months. Not only had she met his friends, she'd been invited into their circle, she was planning a wedding for one of them, and she'd been there for a pregnancy announcement.

Laura pressed her fingers to her eyes. This was more than the stupid house. This was more than her business and trying to find the perfect venue to sell. When her abuela called him a good man, and her mother rolled her eyes, she had agreed with her grandmother. Hell, she'd even told her she thought she could love him.

Love. That's what it was.

The noise from the other side of the door, and the light that crept around the trim, told her that Toby had arrived home. She only had moments to pull herself together.

The woman in the suit, in the dark mudroom, didn't uphold her professionalism at the moment. Her hands still shook and her stomach still knotted.

She heard the beeping of the buttons on the door lock, and she righted herself as the door opened.

"Jesus Christ!" Toby's voice was quick and loud. "You scared the shit out of me." He flicked on the light and Laura winced. "What are you doing?"

Laura looked up at him. His towering frame, dark hair and beard, and those deep, dark eyes sucked her in.

He hung his commuter bag on a hook on the wall and walked toward her, taking her shoulders in his hands.

"You're freaking me out. What happened?" he asked as he looked down at her.

"I love you." The words tumbled from her mouth, directly from her heart.

Toby's eyes widened and then softened as a smile tugged at the corners of his mouth. "Say it again."

"I love you."

"Again," he pleaded as he let his hands fall to her hips and he hoisted her up and set her on the counter next to the dryer.

Laura yelped as her legs brushed the cold countertop, then wrapped around him as he stepped in even closer.

"I love you."

Toby pulled the pins from her hair and let the bun fall loose around her shoulders. His fingers skimmed her throat, followed by kisses.

"Again."

She couldn't help but tuck her fingers up and into his hair, letting her head fall back to expose her throat to him more. "I love you."

Toby sent small pulses of electricity through her as he grazed her collar bone with his lips. Each zap had her tightening her legs around him.

"I love you, Toby Maxwell. I love you," she repeated again, her voice airy and filled with lust.

His mouth came to hers as his fingers lifted into her hair.

"I never thought I'd hear you say those words," his breath was warm in her ear. "I wasn't sure how patient I could be."

Laura eased back. "What do you mean?"

"I've loved you since the moment I saw you."

She laughed as she pressed her forehead to his. "You wanted

to have me charged with trespassing."

"I did. But I would have bailed you out and brought you home with me." He nipped her nose with a kiss. "I fell in love with you in that no-nonsense suit and hairstyle. I fell in love with the brashness that would have you drive up to someone's house and take pictures. I fell in love with your energy."

"I thought it might have been the see-through cami I wore the next time I showed up alone."

Toby brushed another kiss to her jaw. "That's when I knew I couldn't keep my hands off you," he confessed as he cupped her breasts in his hands. "Tell me again."

"I love you," she sighed as his mouth came to hers and he lifted her from the counter and her legs stayed wrapped around him.

"I'm never going to get tired of hearing that."

Laura lifted her head to look down into his eyes. "I've never said it to anyone that wasn't family."

Toby started up the stairs, but stopped, lowering them both down so that she was beneath him on a step, and he balanced himself with one hand on the railing and one next to her.

"I'm the first person you've fallen in love with?"

"Yes," she admitted.

"Will your family be okay with us?"

Laura narrowed her eyes on him. "Why are you bringing them up now?"

"Because, I want you to move in with me and I know their opinion will matter to you."

Laura let out a breath. "Move in with you?"

"I want you with me always. I don't want to spend another day without you."

With her back pressed against the step, Laura looked up at the chandelier above the entryway to the majestic house that had brought her into Toby's life in the first place. How was it possible that in under a month she had the ultimate invitation?

CHAPTER 38

*L*aura hadn't slept in her own bed for a week, and she hadn't committed to moving in with Toby either, but she couldn't stay away.

She'd been smart enough to take a suit from work home with her each night that she went to Toby's so she didn't have to make multiple stops. There was a small salon room in the back of the house where her bridal business thrived, and she would do her hair and makeup each morning there. For some reason, she was afraid to go home—afraid she'd want to stay in the comfort of it and not go back to Toby's.

But there would be a time she'd have to go home and she'd have to make her decision on living arrangements. Though part of her couldn't just abandon what she'd worked so hard for. Common sense said she could rent her house and live at Toby's. It would be a source of income, and just in case, it would be there when she needed it.

Laura held the eyeliner to her eye, then lowered it as she looked into the mirror. The words *I love you* had begun to flow freely between them in the past week, since she'd sprung them on him in the mudroom. But they hadn't revisited his proposal about living together. Perhaps he was just giving her time to think.

"The bakery is on the phone for you," Irene said, standing in the doorway to the salon room. "And is everything in order in here? Misty is coming to do a bridal hair consult."

Laura looked around the room. "It's ready, and I'll get the call in just a moment."

"You're glowing, you know," Irene said smiling.

Laura turned to her. "What do you mean?"

"I've known you since college. I've never seen you radiate the same happiness that your clients do. I've never seen you in love, Laura. That's what I'm talking about."

Laura made an O shape with her mouth, but no sound came out. "I told him I loved him last week."

Irene's smile widened. "I knew the day that enormous bouquet arrived he was the one."

"I don't know about that."

"Oh, I do," Irene said, still grinning at her.

"I don't know how to handle it."

"You should. You're an expert at it. Look how many people you deal with who have the same stars in their eyes."

"And look how many of them spend money on something fancy and then it doesn't last a year."

Irene nodded in agreement. "And you know exactly which of those couples are like that." Irene tapped her hand on the door-jamb then walked away.

Laura turned back to the mirror and studied herself. She did know what couples were like that. And they usually got together when one of them sought out the other for personal gains.

Thursday night guys' night had turned into everyone coming to Toby's house to sample wedding cake.

Toby had watched Laura flit around the kitchen for hours. There were boxes of cake pieces, each of a different flavor and color. All he could think about was Charlotte and Connor's reactions when they saw that much cake.

Their friends, he thought of them now as theirs, wouldn't arrive for another half hour. He wanted to drag Laura away for a few minutes for his own needs, but she was focused on what she was doing. And what she was doing was making his kitchen look as if it were ready for a wedding.

The small finger napkins were imprinted with *Laura Torres Weddings*. Small plastic plates, which he assumed were disposable, but they sure were pretty, were rimmed with gold and had matching lettering.

There was a bottle of champagne in a bucket of ice, and he'd seen her put sparkling cider in the refrigerator for children and nursing and expectant mothers.

Two flutes for the champagne had gold ribbon tied on their stems. They were etched with the words *Bride* and *Groom*.

Pads of paper and pens were laid out on the counter with the cake flavors and colors, presumably so everyone could mark their favorite flavors.

Balloons, in weighted bouquets, decorated each end of the island, and he wondered if the colors were what Sarah had picked for their wedding.

"I can honestly say, I never thought my house would look like this," Toby grinned from his position in the doorway to the mudroom as he leaned up against the doorjamb.

"The kitchen at my office gets decorated like this for cake tasting. Of course, this is on a much bigger scale," she said without looking up, but continuing to tend to some detail he didn't understand.

"They're all going to flip."

A smile formed on her lips and she looked up at him. "Wait until you see what your house will look like."

And that, he thought, still scared the hell out of him.

Laura rearranged forks and plastic wine glasses. "Sarah would like the Christmas decor to still be up for the wedding."

"Well, it should be. It'll only be the day after."

"Yes, but that was an option to have it taken down."

Toby nodded. "Let me guess, my regular tree in the game room isn't going to be enough decoration, is it?"

Laura stopped what she was doing. "You don't decorate for Christmas with more than one tree?"

"A silver antique in the corner of the basement."

She nodded slowly. "I'm glad I realized that in August."

"Never gave it too much thought. I usually go home for Christmas."

"Oh, I hadn't thought of that either."

Toby moved to her now that he seemed to have deflated the energy that Laura had been buzzing about with. He pulled her to him.

"I thought about it right away when Sarah asked to use my house. I've already made plans to have my family come out after the wedding and we'll do Christmas after the fact."

"They don't mind?"

"Why would they? I asked and they said yes."

She nodded slowly, then pressed her hand to her chest. "I suppose I'll need to make sure everything is in order before Christmas, so that I can still be at my parents'."

"I'll bet your mother and grandmother put on an impressive spread."

There was a spark in her eyes again. "They do. Will you be there?"

Toby brushed his thumb over her cheek. "Do you want me there?"

Laura licked her lips and nodded. "I do. Though, I have to admit, I'm very selfish about it. Christmas has always been me and my family. I've never had to share a holiday."

"Every couple has to share."

"Right. In time, they'll understand that, right?"

"In time, even traditions change. People join families, children are born, family members die."

She pulled from him and moved a stack of napkins and then back again. "We're really rushing everything, aren't we? It's mid-August and eighty degrees outside, and we're making Christmas plans."

"Because I still plan to be the one you say you love at Christmas."

She turned back to him now and lifted her arms around his neck. "I do love you and I will still love you at Christmas."

They had nearly four months before Sarah's wedding. An entire lifetime could happen in those four months. The past four weeks had proven that. Who would have thought that Toby would have fallen in love in four weeks and bet his entire future on it?

CHAPTER 39

$\mathcal{L}$aura sat at her desk scrolling through the meetings in her calendar and upcoming weddings. She looked through the checklists for weddings that were to be held before the end of the year. Specifically, she looked over Sarah and Bruce's list.

Because she'd had a personal interest in the wedding, namely Toby's house, they were ahead of schedule with all of the plans. Sarah had picked out the linens and floral arrangements. They'd had the cake tasting in Toby's kitchen, which had been a huge success.

She laughed when she thought about it. They had all eaten enough cake to be sick, and she'd even taken some to her family's for dinner on Sunday. But it had been a magical night. A night where she showed off her business, and she hadn't even realized that was what she was doing until Toby had complimented her on it.

And then there was the moment at midnight, when she and Toby had walked to the kitchen, naked, and shared a piece of cake which they had then smeared over one another.

Her temperature rose just thinking about it.

That had been a month ago. Since then, she'd done many tastings, and none of them would ever compare.

Save the date cards had been sent out for Sarah and Bruce's wedding. And just that morning, the woman who did the calligraphy for Laura's clients, delivered their invitations, which would go out the second week of October.

The last thing Sarah had to decide on was her dress, and they had a day planned, with all of the women, to search for the perfect dress.

Rachel and Catherine had already been in touch with her about a bridal shower and a bachelorette party. They knew they were competing with the holidays, so they thought they'd better get planning. Toby had convinced her that they'd asked her to help plan the events as a friend—a member of their inner circle—but she still couldn't help but wonder why she felt as if they just wanted her expertise.

Irene tapped on Laura's office door. "There's a Mr. Best on the phone for you. He says he's a realtor returning your call." Irene's voice held the tone of a question and Laura nodded.

"Thank you."

"Are you moving?" This time she asked her straight out, and Laura laughed.

"I need to take the call."

"And I need to know if you're upgrading your bedroom."

Laura tucked her lips between her teeth. Irene was much more than her assistant, she'd been her confidant since college, even though they didn't share the same kind of relationship Rachel shared with Catherine.

"I'll let you know," Laura said as she shooed Irene out of the office.

∽

Laura walked into Toby's house, balancing a box in her arms. The aroma that hit her had her stomach growling. The music was loud and she could hear him singing.

She set the box on the island before he noticed her and then commanded the speaker to turn down the volume.

"I guess I had that a bit loud. I didn't hear you come in."

Laura laughed as she walked toward him and kissed him. "What are you making?"

"Sun dried tomato pasta with chicken," he said as he pulled the pins from her hair which held her bun in place.

Laura closed her eyes as he loosened the strands and ran his fingers through it. Then, with his fingers curled in her hair, he pressed his lips to her throat and she moaned as she gripped his belt loops to steady herself.

When he eased back, Toby glanced at the box on the island. "What did you bring?"

"I stopped by my house and packed up a box."

Toby lifted his hand to her face and brushed his thumb over her cheek. "You brought a box. You've been here every night for the past month. Is this your very subtle way of telling me you're moving in—finally?"

"I take my time when I make my decisions." She giggled, taking his hand from her cheek and pressing a kiss to his palm. "Well, on some things."

Toby turned to the stove and turned off the heat. "I didn't expect to feel as giddy about it as I do."

"Giddy?"

"Sue me for having feelings," he teased. "I want you here."

"I talked to a real estate agent today and he's going to manage my property and I'm going to rent it out."

"Your house? You're renting out your house?"

"It's too much of a business opportunity to sell it."

Now he laughed. "We're so much alike." He kissed her hard on the mouth. "I love you. This makes me happy."

"I know I've basically lived here for a month, but I'm scared to death."

"It's going to be perfect." He kissed her again. "We're okay to tell your family about it at dinner this weekend?"

"If you don't mind, I'm going to go over tomorrow and let them know."

She saw the flash of irritation in his eyes, but the smile remained on his lips.

"Whatever works for you," he said as he pulled her in closer, then took her hand and began to lead her out of the kitchen. "C'mon."

"Where are we going? Finish cooking," she laughed as he tugged her toward the stairs.

"I have to show you something."

Laura was surprised that when they cleared the top of the staircase, Toby passed by his bedroom and walked to the end of the hallway. Pushing open the door to a room she'd never even been in, they stepped inside the dark room.

Toby moved to the window and opened the blinds, letting in the light from the setting sun.

"What do you think?"

Laura looked around the empty room. "I think your house is too big if you have rooms that are closed off and empty."

"Don't take it wrong if I tell you that you sound like my mother." He moved back to her and gathered her hands in his. "I want you to have it."

"So when you asked me to move in with you, you didn't mean live with you or sleep with you?"

Toby laughed. "I mean for your office." Taking her hand again, he led her to the window which faced southwest, and the view of the mountains greeted her. "I know that every evening you take out your laptop and finish your day's work. On Sundays you gather all the data you need from the weddings over the weekend. On Thursdays, even if you're having nachos and margaritas, you're finalizing plans for the weekend's weddings. I want you to make this your space in *our* home to do all of that."

Tears stung her eyes. "Toby, this is very sweet."

"I want you here and I want you to be comfortable. And I promise to never threaten to have you arrested again."

She laughed as she wrapped her arms around him and rested her head to his chest. That fateful night, Laura had only hoped to get close to the house. She never would have imagined that less than three months later she'd be living in it.

CHAPTER 40

*L*aura gathered the bouquet of flowers from the passenger seat of her car and climbed out. As she closed the door, she looked up at the home where her parents lived.

Her mother had wanted that house since Laura was a little girl. It had been owned by the man who owned the bowling alley Laura's grandfather had worked at. When the man had died, Laura approached his son and offered to buy the house.

It wasn't until that moment had she realized she'd over-stepped her boundaries more than once when it came to real estate. She'd done the same thing when the building she had her bridal business in had been gutted by fire.

"What are you doing outside just looking up at the house?"

Laura turned when she heard her father's voice from the driveway.

She smiled and walked to him, hugging him when he reached out his arms. "I was just thinking about all the houses that mean something to me."

He lifted a brow and studied her. "You have a good eye for real estate."

Sure, she thought. That was it.

"Where is your fancy boyfriend?"

Laura and her father walked to the back of the house with their arms around each other. "He's home. I told him I wanted to come alone tonight."

"You're having problems?"

"No, *Papito*. We're not having problems."

As they reached the back door, her father turned her toward him. "I like him."

"I do too," she said, smiling up at him.

"But I won't tolerate him not being good to you."

"He's very good to me."

Her father pressed his hand to her cheek. "Good. You deserve to have a man love you."

"He does love me."

He pressed a kiss to her forehead. "I can tell. So why are you here unannounced with flowers?"

Laura opened the door. "C'mon."

She stepped into her parents' house and her mother was in the kitchen, apron on, baking bread.

"*Mona*," her mother moved to her, calling her monkey, as she and her grandmother always did.

Laura kissed her mother's cheek. "*Mamá*, these are for you," she said handing her mother the bouquet.

There was no smile on her mother's lips as she'd hoped. "What's wrong?"

"Nothing."

"You showed up on a Wednesday with flowers. What happened to you?"

Laura's father stepped between them. "Let's sit down," he encouraged them.

Laura pulled out a chair at the kitchen table and sat. Her father pulled out another chair, then offered the seat to her mother before taking a seat.

"I don't know why you think I'm here with bad news," Laura adjusted her watch and messed with the bracelet on her wrist.

"Because you're my daughter," her mother said cradling the flowers.

"Then you should assume I'm here for something good."

Laura's father covered her hand with his large one. "What do you have to tell us, *mona*?"

Drawing in a breath of courage, she reminded herself that she was in her thirties and shouldn't have to worry about what she was about to tell them.

"I talked to a realtor yesterday about managing my house. I'm going to rent it out."

Her mother's eyes narrowed. "That's a silly thing to do. You love your house. Do you need money?"

"No, *Mamá*." Laura drew in another breath. "I'm moving in with Toby."

That caused her mother to rise, carrying the flowers to the sink.

Laura and her father exchanged looks before Laura stood and walked toward her mother.

"You have something to say about this," Laura led her into the argument she knew was coming.

"You're going to move in with a man?"

"Not just any man."

Her mother let out a low groan as she began to pull the paper from the bouquet. "He's a man. He only wants one thing from my little girl. And he hasn't asked you to marry him, only to move in with him. That's not right."

Laura moved in closer to her mother. "I'm old enough to know what any man wants from me. And I'm old enough to be in love with a man who treats me right and wants to share his home with me."

Her mother shook her head as she rearranged the flowers in

her hand. "No man should expect you to live with him and not marry you."

"We're not to that place in our relationship yet."

"But you'll live with him in sin?"

Laura's father stood now and walked toward her mother, placing his hands on her shoulders. "You need to let her speak her mind."

"It's wrong," her mother sobbed now.

"It's not our place to shame her for her decisions," Laura heard him whisper in her ear. "It's our place to support her."

Laura's mother laid the flowers on the counter and walked back to the table without looking at her. When her father nodded toward Laura, she knew that was his way of saying she should sit down and continue her conversation.

"*Mamá*, this isn't to hurt you," Laura said as she sat next to her mother. "I love Toby."

"And he's not man enough to come here and support you telling me you're going to live in sin?"

"I asked him not to come. I knew what your reaction would be."

Now her mother looked at her, her eyes narrow. "If you knew, then you knew it was because this is a sin."

"I knew because you believe it's a sin. *Mamá*, I don't think that way. I think this is a wonderful opportunity to live with the man who makes me happy. I love him, *Mamá*. I want to be with him every day. And someday, maybe we'll get married. For now, we want to take this step."

Her mother wiped tears from her cheek. "You always make things harder."

Laura swallowed hard. When her mother couldn't justify something different than what she believed in, then she said it was Laura making it harder. But Laura had long ago learned that it was her mother's processing a situation. In time, she'd come around, and if Laura just let that happen, there wouldn't be weeks in which they didn't speak.

Laura's father stood behind her mother rubbing her shoulders. "She's old enough to make these decisions," he defended Laura. "Look at what she's done in her life. What she's done for all of us," he reminded her mother.

After a few moments, her mother raised her damp eyes to look up at her. "You're not pregnant, are you?"

"No." Laura shook her head.

"You know you're getting older. You should think about marriage and babies." Her mother wiped at her eyes.

Laura wrapped her arms around her mother. Old beliefs and bits of outdated religion held her mother captive from true happiness sometimes. But knowing how much she loved Laura, it made it easier to understand why something joyous would always become an argument.

CHAPTER 41

*W*hen Toby pushed the button on the garage door, he saw Laura's car was already parked inside. He'd worked late because he'd expected Laura to be at her parents' house much later.

He parked his car and as he opened his car door, he could hear music blaring from inside. Laughing, he grabbed his commuter bag, and walked into the house.

Toby hung up his bag, and noticed there were more boxes stacked by the base of the staircase. There were no lights on upstairs, and Laura wasn't in the kitchen, so Toby started downstairs to find her.

The lights were on in the gym and he could hear the unmistakable sound of shoes on the treadmill. Not wanting to startle her, he instructed the speakers to turn down their volume before stepping into the gym.

On the floor was a yoga mat and a set of free weights, and Laura was pressing the button on the treadmill to take her from a full run to a slow jog.

"I didn't expect you to be home," Toby said loud enough to be heard over the treadmill and music.

Laura stopped the treadmill, and stood with her hands on the railing sucking in breaths.

"Well, I'm home."

Toby crossed his arms and leaned against the doorjamb. "I'm going to assume things didn't go well."

Laura picked up the towel she had next to her and wiped her face, but Toby knew it wasn't just sweat she wiped away, there were also tears.

"It's a sin," she said through a sob. "I have a college education, own a very successful business with a full staff, own my house, own my car, and am in my freaking thirties, but I want to live with a man and it's a sin."

"But I saw you brought more boxes."

"Because I'm going to live here," she said certainly.

"I'm glad to hear that."

"Then she asked me if I was pregnant, as if that's the only reason to move in with a man."

"And what did you tell her?"

Laura raised a brow and a laugh broke through. "Why would I tell her anything but no?"

Toby shrugged, because for the first time in his life, he didn't think it sounded like a horrible consequence.

Laura moved to him and he wrapped his arms around her.

"Then in her next breath, she told me that I wasn't getting any younger, so I should think about getting married and having kids."

Now Toby laughed as he pressed a kiss to her head. "I guess we have a lot to think about."

Laura eased back and looked up at him. "Some other time. Right now, I'm committing to moving in here. I'm not ready to talk about marriage and kids. I'm still trying to figure out why I'm here."

Toby raised his hand to her cheek. "You're here because I love you."

She rested her head against his chest again. "Thank you. That's exactly what I wanted to hear."

~

Alex opened the front door, Celia Rose on his hip. "Tell me you remembered the poker chips," he said, and Toby lifted the case he carried.

"It's funny that you plan guys' night with poker, and you don't have anything."

Alex shrugged. "Ray had a poker table top to put on the card table. Bruce brought the beer and Craig picked up pizza. Seriously all I have to do now is open the door when you all get here."

Toby laughed as he walked through the door, taking a moment to tap Celia Rose's nose.

Bruce walked out of the kitchen with a beer in each hand. He handed one to Toby. "I had Sarah drop me off after we did a walkthrough on the new house. Can I get a ride home later?"

Toby nodded as he took the beer Bruce offered. "I suppose. It's not too far out of my way," Toby teased.

Bruce tapped his beer to Toby's. "You're an upstanding guy," Bruce laughed.

"Walkthrough, huh? Your house is done then?"

"We close on it next week. I can't freaking believe it. A year ago my whole life was shit. Now I'm employed, buying a house, and I managed to get Alex's sister."

Alex shook his head. "Obviously my wishes mean nothing to you."

"Not a damned thing," Bruce agreed as he held out his hands to Celia Rose, and she leapt into her future uncle's arms. He turned to Toby with his niece in his arms. "I hear you're getting a new roommate."

"I am."

Alex slapped him on the back. "We've all made it look so good, he snatched the first woman he's talked to in years."

Bruce shook his head. "I seem to remember he had two women on his arms last New Year's Eve."

Toby coughed. "And you could see me with women while you were hiding with Alex's sister?"

Alex took the chips from Toby and leaned in toward Bruce. "Yeah, asshole," he whispered but laughed as he walked past his best friend and future brother-in-law.

Bruce shrugged and then kissed his niece on the head. "He still loves me."

"You're lucky he didn't kill you."

"I am. But really, you and the wedding gal? She's moving in?"

"Laura," Toby said as if to remind him of her name. "And yeah, she's moving in."

"I'll bet she's super happy about that."

"I hope so."

"I mean she had eyes on your house and now you've invited her in. That's a good deal for her," Bruce teased as he turned and carried Celia Rose away.

Toby sipped his beer. He was used to being razzed by his friends, but that had stung. Was that what they all thought of Laura? That she was some kind of gold-digger, or house digger as the case may be. Well that wasn't what Toby thought at all. And he'd make sure that any of those assholes knew that if they mentioned it again.

CHAPTER 42

"Girls' night is at my place in two weeks!" Sarah shouted over the noise at the restaurant as she lifted her margarita up in salute.

The women at the table all lifted their glasses of water and iced tea to celebrate with her. All except Laura, whose attention was directed down at her phone.

Rachel nudged her. "We're celebrating here," she said playfully.

Laura looked up and saw what was going on. She quickly picked up her margarita and held it over the center of the table.

"I'm sorry. What are we celebrating?" she asked.

Sarah laughed as they all pulled back their drinks and sipped. "We close on our house next week. So in a week, I'll be out of Toby's hair for good."

Laura nodded behind her margarita glass, then sipped.

Kelly leaned in next to her. "You're a million miles away. Is everything okay?"

Laura bit down on her bottom lip and looked around the table. Where she hadn't been paying attention to anyone, now all eyes were on her.

"Just work, and family," she said playfully. "You know, when it rains…"

There were tears stinging her eyes when she said it, and she knew they'd all seen it because the women swarmed.

Rachel's hand came to Laura's arm. Kelly scooted her chair closer to wrap an arm around Laura's shoulders. Catherine filled Laura's half empty glass of water and handed it to her, and Sarah handed her a napkin to wipe her eyes.

"I'm sorry. That came out of nowhere," Laura's voice shook as the threatening tears fell.

Rachel shook her head. "No, not from nowhere. Something is building up in there. You're in a safe place. You can share with us —if you want to."

Laura dabbed at the tears, forever careful of her makeup. "I think I'm just overwhelmed. My life has been going at full speed for months."

Rachel nodded. "But a lot of that has been wonderful stuff, right?"

Nodding, Laura let out a breath. She looked around the table at the women who had become her friends.

Rachel smiled. "We're all ears."

"Are you sure?"

Four heads bobbed up and down in solidarity.

"For starters, my mother is a bit old fashioned," she said, thinking it would be all she had to say, but she had more. "Let's forget that I'm in my thirties, and have a successful business which I built from the ground up, and I own the building we're housed out of." She took a breath. "I also bought my parents a house, and made sure my grandmother was in good care. And I did all of that out of the goodness of my heart, not because they asked, but because they had all worked so hard to give me a good life."

"You're grateful," Rachel said.

"I am. I see what they went through to just survive, and they gave me the best education and opportunity that they couldn't have for themselves. But old traditions and beliefs have my mother at odds with me because I want to live in sin with a man."

The women nodded as if at some point they too had had this conversation with their mothers.

Kelly ran her hand over the only slight swell of her belly. "I sometimes think that's why Ray and I got married when we did. Don't mind that we'd lived with each other on and off during college—well unofficially. And I'd been having sex with him, but mention shacking up when we graduated, and my mother blew a gasket."

They all laughed.

"I snuck Bruce into the house last year," Sarah said and the laughter continued. "I'd never done something like that. We were sneaking around in Alex's basement…"

Catherine cleared her throat and Sarah chuckled as she covered Catherine's hand with hers.

"Okay, we were sneaking around in Alex and Catherine's basement," she corrected. "And I snuck him into my mother's house when I was living there, too. Seriously, my mother knew how I felt about him. Alex was the only one who would have killed us. But, yeah, no one was all too happy when he moved into Toby's guest house and I went along."

Laura sipped her margarita. "I'm not sure what they all think. Women in their thirties aren't *pristine*. We've had lovers. We've made mistakes."

Kelly picked up her iced tea. "Speaking as the mother with the oldest children, you want to believe that no matter what, your children need you and your opinions. Having been in your shoes, I can see where I'll do the same things to my kids. We're programmed that way, and I think it makes us, as mothers, feel as if we did something wrong when it's not *by the book*," she said using air-quotes.

Laura smiled at her new circle of friends. "So I should love my mother and not worry."

They each picked up their glasses in salute again.

Rachel set her water glass back on the table. "What else? You said work too."

Nodding, Laura picked up her phone and looked down at it. "Are you all familiar with the Grayson-Miller Mansion?"

Catherine picked up a chip from the nacho plate. "That's a beautiful place. I think I went to a wedding there a few years ago."

"Well, it burnt down about six hours ago," Laura said.

"I saw the smoke," Rachel said. "Now I know where that place was."

Sarah scooped up a chip. "Did you have things planned there?"

Laura nodded. "Four different weddings and a bridal shower. I just got the text that the building is a total loss."

"Ouch," Kelly said. "Now what?"

"I don't know. The bridal shower is only a few weeks away. The first wedding was supposed to be New Year's Eve."

"There's only one choice," Sarah said as she picked up another chip. "Toby's house is as big, and as nice as that other place."

Laura shook her head. "A month ago that would have been exactly what I would have thought. But no, I can't ask him to do that," she said, even though she knew it might be the only way to save her business.

CHAPTER 43

*R*ay threw the ball in from the side of the court and
Bruce took it down to the net. Connor stood under
the net. Bruce bounced the ball in his direction, then scooped
him up to let him sink the ball in the net, then hang from the rim.

"Mom! Mom!" Connor yelled and Kelly lifted her head to see
her son dangling from the rim.

"Well done," she said, but Toby saw her cringe as he dropped
into Bruce's waiting hands.

Connor ran toward his mother after Bruce set him on the
ground. Sarah then jumped on Bruce's back and planted a noisy
kiss to his cheek. "I kicked your ass again," she cheered.

Bruce shook his head as he carried his fiancée toward the
bench.

"Where's your woman today?" Sarah called back to Toby.

"She needed to work," he said, and he heard the sadness in his
voice. There had been no talking her into going to the game
with him.

"That was quite a blow to her business," Sarah said as Bruce
set her down.

Catherine packed up Celia Rose's toys into the backpack she

had. "I can't imagine having to reschedule that many events. And what about all of the invitations that were sent out already?"

Kelly mimicked Catherine's actions, as she too packed up items her children had been entertaining themselves with. "People have to understand. I mean, this kind of stuff happens."

Toby listened to the banter going on around him. Why did it appear that he was the only one that had no idea what they were talking about?

Laura had closed the blinds in the bedroom that Toby had gifted her as an office space. She hadn't taken him too seriously, and hadn't planned for any furniture, but there would be time. As it was, she was seated at a card table on a folding chair with her laptop illuminating the room.

She easily could have gone into the office to work. She'd spent many Sundays there while her weekend team unpacked from Saturday weddings, or prepared Sunday weddings.

Today though, she needed peace and quiet.

She had called every anxious bride on Thursday, the moment she'd heard about the fire. Luckily, she'd waited until she'd heard it was a total loss, so she could shut down any thoughts of waiting out reconstruction. Laura wasn't big on hoping a location would be ready.

The tapping at the door had her jumping, and when the light filtered in from the hallway, she winced against it.

Toby stood there in his basketball shorts, his hair damp from sweat.

"Everything okay in here?" he asked, never moving to enter the room.

"It's fine. I'm fine," she said quickly, and realized she might have had too much coffee.

Toby walked into the room and held out his hand as if asking her to take it.

"I'm really busy," she said.

"I need five minutes of your time."

Laura looked at the computer screen and the list of things she needed to do. Entire weddings had to be replanned and he needed her time. This was why she'd never been in a relationship.

Reluctantly, she took his hand and he led her out of the room and down the hall to the bedroom.

She certainly didn't have time for this.

Toby walked them to the bathroom. He let go of her hand and turned on the shower. As it heated, he began to strip out of his basketball clothes, depositing them in the hamper next to the shower.

Laura looked at her watch. Though appreciative of the show, she had things to do.

"What are you working on?" he asked as he took a towel from the cabinet and hung it on the hook near the shower.

"Work. I don't have time to go into all the details."

He nodded slowly. "Yeah, I get it. I don't know how many weekends I've lost to things not going to plan."

Laura worried her lip as he pulled open the glass shower door, tested the water, and then stepped inside. "Who said things weren't going as planned?"

"I just assumed…"

She blew out a breath. And now she knew why she didn't have a tight knit group of girlfriends either.

"What did the girls say to you?"

He chuckled as he pumped soap into his hand. "Honestly, they didn't say a damn thing to me. I told Sarah you were working, and then this coded message came from everyone else. Something about rescheduling lots of weddings."

Laura's defenses kicked in much faster than her respect for

the women. But she quickly realized she hadn't specifically told them not to say anything. And, the fire had been well publicized.

Tears stung her eyes now. She hadn't meant to keep anything secret from Toby, she just wasn't used to sharing her business with anyone.

Laura looked down at herself. Still dressed in yoga pants and a tank top, which she noticed had a coffee stain, she began to slip out of her clothes.

Tossing them into the same hamper Toby had thrown his clothes into, she pulled the band from her hair and let it fall.

Pulling open the glass shower door, she stepped into the warm water spray, which came from three different directions. Laura wrapped her arms around Toby and pressed her cheek to his back.

"I'm sorry," she said.

"Why are you sorry?" he asked as he turned and wrapped her in his arms.

"I don't know how to share my joy or my misery."

"What's going on?"

Toby tipped her head back into the stream of water and wet her hair.

"One of my venues burnt down on Thursday."

He filled his hand with shampoo and turned her away from him so he could massage it into her hair. "That mansion?"

"Yes."

"And you had weddings booked there?"

"Yes."

"And now you have to reschedule?"

"Yes," her voice had begun to tremble. "There's rescheduling, finding similar venues, sending out new announcements and invitations, and recovering from the financial loss of deposits that were made."

Toby turned her again and tipped her head back to rinse the shampoo out of her hair. "That's a lot to think about."

"It is. But I have insurance on weddings for things like this."

"That's a solid business practice." He turned her around again, and this time pumped conditioner into his hand and massaged it into her hair. "What will you do?"

"I'm so booked out, I have to find venues that are similar and can take us on those days."

His hands left her hair and ran over her shoulders. "You'll figure it all out. You wouldn't have gotten this far without knowing who to punt." He turned her toward him. "Let me know where I can help you." He pressed a kiss to her lips. "I love you. I'd do *anything* to help you."

CHAPTER 44

*I*rene set stacks of files on the table in the design room and everyone filed into the room. Mondays were usually quiet. Tux returns and follow-ups didn't usually warrant the entire staff being in the design room around the conference table, but this wasn't any regular Monday.

Laura had catered breakfast as an incentive to have everyone show up. She looked at her notes and began their meeting.

The Grayson-Miller Mansion had been booked for four of their weddings and one bridal shower. And though it wasn't a large number, there were very few venues of that size that hadn't already been booked, or then were booked up by other weddings that needed to shift as well.

Laura informed her staff that she had personally talked to each bride. They were gratefully understanding, but she knew that was only shock. The last thing she wanted was any bride to decide to take her business elsewhere.

This wasn't the first time they'd had to reschedule, but it was the first time they had to reschedule that many weddings at one time.

"So I'm open to suggestions," she said after having shared the details with her team.

The room went silent for a moment as each of them exchanged glances. Then Amy walked around the room and pulled the photo off of Sarah's board.

"What about this house?" she asked, holding up the picture Laura had taken the day she'd met Toby.

"No," Laura's answer was swift and stern.

"I heard some guy axed some girl there and had another kidnapped and ready to kill too," one of her younger staff members blurted out and the entire room broke out into sporadic conversation.

"Whoa!" Laura came out of her chair and put her hands flat on the table. As she'd never had any kind of outburst like that, everyone in the room went quiet, and eyes widened. "No more of that. Nothing like that happened in that house," her voice was strained. "Now let's focus. We have four weddings and a bridal shower to reschedule. We need venues that hold the same number of people and ones with dates that will accommodate."

"She's right. That house would be perfect," the voice came from the doorway and all heads turned.

Heat rose in Laura's cheeks when she saw Toby standing there. Had he seriously just interrupted her meeting and offered his house?

At that moment, Laura's stomach knotted and she thought she might just get sick.

"If you wouldn't mind waiting in my office," she growled at Toby, "we need to finish our meeting."

Dismissing her staff with that same bite in her voice that she'd had when she spoke to Toby, she walked back to her office. Toby stood in the doorway, and when she walked through, he closed the door behind him. Laura plopped down in her desk chair and turned the opposite direction, so anyone looking in, and Toby, couldn't see her face.

"You need to leave, right now," she growled through gritted teeth.

"First of all, I'm not going anywhere, and what's with the mood?" His voice was light and filled with positivity.

"Why aren't you at work?" she asked without turning to look at him.

"I had a meeting around the corner so I thought I stop in."

"Well you should go now."

"Laura," she heard his voice grow nearer.

"I said go!" her voice rose, and she took a breath to try and control her anger. "I'm not turning around, because multiple things will happen. I'm angry right now, and my team doesn't need to see me have any more outbursts."

"Well you did correct her. No one got axed there." Now his voice was strained, she noted.

"And if I turn around and look at you, I'm going to cry."

"That I've seen," he said as he moved close enough she could smell his cologne. "If you need my house, it's yours to use."

The tears were there now, and there was no stopping them. "Toby, go away."

"I love you. Let me help you through this."

She pressed both of her hands to her mouth and now he appeared in front of her. Obviously not taking her warning to get out.

"Laura," he said kneeling down in front of her. "What is going on? Talk to me."

"I'm not kidding. If you don't get out of here, I'll have you thrown out."

Toby ran his tongue over his teeth. "Looking at you right now, I have no doubt that's exactly what you'd do."

"Consider how mad you were when you caught me taking pictures of your house," she spat out the words and his eyes went wide.

"Got it." Toby stood, but he didn't walk away. "I'm leaving, and you'll know where to find me when you're done being mad and hiding from your employees. I expect I'm going to get an earful, and I'm ready for that. But don't you dare not come home, because I'll search for you. I love you and I'm not going to let you ever just dismiss me without talking it out first."

Laura shifted her eyes to the ground and wiped at her cheeks as Toby turned around and she heard the door open and close behind him.

With her back still to the door, she let the tears freely fall. Two months ago she would have sold her soul to get into Toby Maxwell's house. She drove by it every day, stopped on the side of the road and thought of what she could do with that house. How many hours had she spent searching online about the house and the man?

She should have jumped from her seat and jumped into his arms when he offered his house. He'd said he'd do *anything* to help her. Laura supposed he meant it then.

But the house was her home now. And hadn't Sarah said the only thing he cared more about, aside from his family and friends, was his house and his cars?

Laura's chest ached and she pressed her hand to it.

If she took his offer, then she'd be selling herself for what she'd wanted from the beginning. Hadn't she already considered that the marriages she saw fail did so because someone had ventured into that relationship with an agenda?

Now her breath came in pants and she wasn't so sure she wasn't going to pass out.

When the door opened again, she sat up in her chair, but didn't turn around. "I told you to go!" she shouted again.

"I sent everyone else out on jobs," Irene's voice soothed. "Now why don't you turn around and talk to me."

CHAPTER 45

*I*t was seven o'clock before Laura walked into the house, but it was quiet. Toby's car had been in the garage, but he wasn't in the kitchen, in his office or bedroom, and the game room was dark and quiet.

Laura stepped behind the bar and poured herself a glass of wine. Usually she wouldn't use alcohol to calm her nerves, but today seemed to warrant just that.

As she sipped, she realized the patio door was open. Stepping outside, she noticed Toby in the pool, swimming laps.

She sat down in one of the patio chairs that looked out over the manicured back yard with its colors absorbing autumn.

Laura watched Toby swim from one end of the pool to the other over and over again. She'd finished her wine before he finally came to the edge of the pool and looked up toward her as if maybe he'd sensed her.

He lifted himself from the pool, wrapped in a robe, and started up the walk toward her.

Laura's mouth went dry watching him near her. She couldn't see his eyes in the glow of the setting sun, but she imagined they were filled with anger. Laura didn't blame him if he was angry, but she was ready to hold her own.

As he neared, Laura set her glass on the table next to her.

When Toby reached her, he held out his hands, pulled her to her feet, and kissed her as if no angry words had been spoken between them.

He smelled of chlorine and his face was damp. Toby pulled her closer, deepening the kiss until she wrapped her arms around his neck and he hoisted her to his hips.

But he didn't move and carry her off.

When they exhausted their breath, they eased apart, and Toby lowered her to her feet. But he didn't let Laura out of his arms.

"I was killing time until you got home," he said softly, pressing his forehead to hers.

"I was killing time trying to figure out how I was going to react to you when I got home," Laura admitted. "I'm not sure this is how I expected it to go."

"We have a lot to talk about."

"We do," she agreed.

Toby pressed another kiss to her lips. "I'm going to take a quick shower. Why don't you pour us both a glass of wine. I have a meat and cheese board in the refrigerator under the bar."

Laura laughed. "Why do you have that?"

"Just because we need to sit down and talk doesn't mean we shouldn't be able to do it with a little class."

He had a way of easing her worries, Laura thought as she watched him walk into the house and disappear into the bathroom.

Picking up her glass, she walked back into the house. She pulled down another glass behind the bar and filled them both.

Pulling open the small refrigerator under the bar, she laughed as she took out the meat and cheese board, wrapped in plastic wrap.

Laura hadn't dated too many men, but none of them had as much class as Toby—and she rather enjoyed that side of him.

Toby pulled on a pair of lounge pants and a T-shirt that he kept in the cabinet. Running his fingers through his wet hair, he wondered if he had time in his schedule to get a haircut during the week. Usually Toby had it scheduled, but since Laura had happened into his life, he'd let some of those little things slide. Spending time with Laura took priority over the need to have his life meticulously planned out.

Walking out of the bathroom, he turned off the light and walked out toward the bar. Laura wasn't sitting there, as he'd assumed she would be. That was when he noticed her on the patio, the fireplace in the center of the conversation circle flickered. She was still dressed in the suit she'd worn to work, only she'd taken off her shoes. Even her hair was still in the signature bun she wore when she dressed in those suits.

She held her glass of wine in her hand, but her gaze was focused on the mountains. Toby knew her mind was going in a million directions. But now they had to talk about how he could help her.

"You're beautiful," he said as he stepped out onto the patio and Laura looked up at him.

"I appreciate that." She sipped her wine.

Toby took the seat next to her and picked up the wine that waited for him. "Okay, no more bullshit," he said directly, and her eyes moved to his. "How can I help you?"

Laura wrapped her hands around her glass and crossed her legs. "Let's get one thing perfectly clear, I am the only person to make decisions in my business."

"Not hard to understand."

"What you did today undermined my authority."

Toby sipped his wine. He'd like to tell her what he was

thinking in that moment, but he was the one in trouble. Keeping his mouth shut would be a better idea.

"My entire team saw me lose my cool today," she admitted. "I've never done that before."

"I don't know how you've gone that long without an outburst. When you're the boss, it's hard to keep your cool all the time."

"It's very hard," she agreed. "When you showed up and said what you said, well, it came at a very bad time. And I can promise you, I would never—never—show up at one of your meetings and just speak."

Toby felt the air in his lungs deflate. "Saying I'm sorry won't do justice to how I feel right now."

"Just know, I'll never meddle into your business."

He nodded. "And I'll never meddle in yours—again."

Laura set her wine on the table, and began to pull the pins from her hair. "I need to find a venue for those weddings."

Toby took a long sip of his wine and let the silence settle between them before he spoke. "I meant it when I said you could use the house."

"I don't want to discuss that."

"Why?"

"Because I live here too now. I understand your hesitation in even wanting Sarah's wedding here."

He couldn't help but smile at that. "It's a house."

"It's your home—our home."

Toby stood and moved to her. Her hair now draped over her shoulders and caught the light of the fire. Holding his hand out to her, she took it and stood.

Wrapping his arms around her, he pressed his forehead to hers. "Home is wherever you are—wherever our family will be."

Laura tucked in her lips and kept her eyes on his. "Don't talk like that. Not now."

"I can't help it. That's why I want you to use the house. It's what you've always wanted, isn't it?"

"Couples don't work out when one of the partners uses the other for their own personal gain."

"Your business's survival," he reminded her.

"Toby, if I use your house as a venue, it will fulfill one of my biggest dreams, but I'm afraid it'll tear us apart."

He ran his hand over her hair. "I'm not going to allow that."

"As if you get all the say."

"There's only one way around this."

"How?"

"I want to buy in. I want to be your business partner."

CHAPTER 46

*L*aura stepped back from him. Her eyes narrowed and her lips pursed. His comment about wanting to buy in had added insult to injury. "I am not some weak-minded, pathetic woman who needs some man to save her ass, Toby Maxwell."

She turned from him and walked inside the house.

Toby stood there for a moment feeling as if he'd just been punched in the gut. When he could breathe, he followed her inside, and up the stairs.

"Whoa. Don't just walk away from me."

Laura stopped at the top of the stairs and looked down at him. "You can't buy your way in or out of everything. No one knows that better than me." She turned again and he followed.

This time when he caught up with her, she was climbing the stairs toward the bedroom. "Laura, let's talk."

"I'm done talking," she sobbed. "I will find a venue, or I might lose these weddings. But I sure as hell am not going to ask you for your house or your money."

"You didn't ask for either of those things. I offered them."

"Why?" She stepped down until they were eye to eye, but she

was on the step above him. "Why would you do that? From the very beginning, I knew that the only thing you prized was this house. You nearly had me arrested for taking pictures of it. The only reason you agreed to let Sarah have her wedding here was because of what happened to her and your guilt over it."

"C'mon…"

"Admit it. When you saw me climb out of that car that day with her and Bruce, you wanted to tell her no. You didn't want me in your house, especially in that capacity."

He reached for her hand, but she yanked it away.

"Don't you understand that it's all different now?" he pleaded. "The only thing that matters to me now is you."

"No. No I don't understand. I don't understand any of this," she sobbed and fell against him, wrapping her arms around his neck.

Toby grabbed hold of the railing to steady them, then pulled her in close. "Baby, it's all okay. It's all going to be okay," he whispered as he pressed kisses to the top of her head.

"How do you know that?"

He smiled, breathing in the scent of her hair. "Because I love you. And for the first time in my life, my business and my house don't mean a damn thing. You're all that matters to me."

Because Laura was going to work late again on Tuesday trying to place those weddings, and keep her schedule on track, Toby invited the guys over because he needed some insight. This was where, for the first time, his intellect wasn't needed, but his friends' knowledge of handling the opposite sex was.

"I don't know what to do for her," Toby said as he lined up his shot on the pool table. "She has four weddings she has to rebook for the same dates in the same sized venue."

"Why same dates?" Bruce asked as he watched Toby's ball miss its mark.

"For one, brides want certain dates."

"That's fair. I suppose Sarah was easygoing there. She took the first opening."

"That's the other thing. Laura's business is steady. She's booked out. She can't do lots of weddings on one day and give the same kind of attention to the couple getting married."

Bruce lined up his shot. "And that matters to her. I know that first-hand."

"Right."

Ray chalked the end of his stick. "What's wrong with your house? It's every bit as big as that mansion."

The comparison stung. The truth was, Toby's house was bigger, but the sting came from knowing the house had once been a trophy, and now it didn't seem to matter as much.

"The fact that I initially didn't want to tell Sarah yes to using it, that seems to weigh heavily on Laura's mind."

Bruce stepped back from the table where he'd been lining up a shot. "You were going to tell Sarah no?"

"Dude, think about it. Think about me and this house. How long did I live here before I finally had all of you to share it with me? Yes, I was like a big selfish kid that didn't want to share my house."

Bruce narrowed his eyes. "Then why tell Sarah yes?"

That sting he'd felt before was starting to burn even more. "She deserves it."

"Because I got a vasectomy and she won't have my kids? Or because someone you employed, whom you didn't personally hire, tried to kill her? If she finds out you let her have her wedding here out of pity and not because you love her as a sister, she'll pull out."

Toby put his cue in the rack and walked around the table to look Bruce in the eye. "And all of that would be why I told her yes. Because when you love someone like a sister, all of that goes into play. So if you make it something different, and she pulls out of having her wedding here, I'll kick your ass."

Bruce dropped his stick to the ground and squared up with Toby. "You couldn't even get a swing in."

"You pushing my buttons makes me think differently," Toby countered.

Alex stepped in, placing a hand on both of their chests. But as he took a breath to scold each of them, it was Laura's voice that came from behind them.

"Are you fighting? Why are you fighting?" she moved toward them, and suddenly Toby thought her presence took over the room, even though she was at least a foot shorter than every man that now surrounded her. "What's going on?"

The vein in Bruce's neck pulsed. "Nothing."

"This isn't nothing," Laura countered and looked up at Toby. "What's going on?"

Toby raked his fingers through his hair. "A little brotherly misunderstanding."

"Over the house?"

Bruce touched her arm, and Toby saw the anger defuse in his eyes. "No. You know what, this isn't over the house. This is over all of us still processing a lot of trauma." He exchanged glances with Toby, then settled his eyes on Laura. "Can I talk to you? Alone?" Again he shot the look toward Toby.

Laura looked at each man, and each of them looked lost in the moment.

"Yes. Why don't we step outside," she offered walking toward the patio door that led to the back yard.

CHAPTER 47

Bruce closed the door behind him as he joined Laura on the patio. She walked out of sight of the doors, and stood in the cool air, her arms wrapped around her.

"By the way, you look very nice," Bruce said.

Laura looked down at her suit. "Thank you. I didn't know you would all be over here tonight."

"Toby needed some brotherly advice, I think." Bruce ran his hand over the back of his neck.

"You think?"

"Listen, he's not a relationship guy." Bruce held his hand up as if to give himself a moment to rethink what he'd said. "He's never really been in one. I guess neither have I, so I'm not sure why I'm here."

"You're in one now," she reminded him, and a smile came to Bruce's lips.

"I am."

"Why were you arguing?"

"It's nothing. You know, it's like I said, we're all still processing a lot of trauma."

Laura brushed a loose strand of hair from her eyes. "I heard you, you know. I know this is over the house."

Bruce nodded and tucked his hands into his pockets. "Listen, that asshole is in love with you."

Laura chuckled. "And doesn't all of that sound lovely wrapped in a package like that?"

That made Bruce chuckle too. "What I mean is, I know why he told Sarah yes to the house. It's what he can do for her. He takes the attack on her and Mindy, and Emily's death, personally. Hell, if anyone should take it personally it should be me. And I did, for a bit. And wouldn't you know it, it was that asshole who helped pull me out of it."

"Again, I'm not sure the description matches the action."

Bruce laughed again. "They're all assholes in my book, if it makes you feel better. But the point is, the house isn't as important to him now that you're in his life. He's worried that if you don't use the house for your weddings, you'll lose them."

Laura pursed her lips. "He dragged you all in on this? This isn't his problem. This is my problem."

Shaking his head, Bruce stepped to her and took her hands. "No. This part I know. When you're a couple, it's not just your problem. If you love him, and I know he loves you, then the problem belongs to both of you."

"It can't be his."

"It is." Bruce smiled down at her. "Sarah and I move out of the guest house this weekend. Maybe you two should take a vacation next week and stay down there. You'd be surprised how different the view is," he said raising his brows and she understood what he was telling her.

"I think he'll miss you being neighbors."

Bruce let out a breath. "I'll forever be grateful to him. He gave me a job when I was unemployed, a home when I needed one, and when he found out about Sarah and me, he didn't rat us out. I'd do anything for that asshole," he said again and she shook her head and laughed. "So here I am, telling you to use the house for the weddings. Love him for who he is and not what he has. And, give him a break. He sucks at this romance stuff."

Yeah, she thought as he moved in to hug Bruce, she was pretty sure she sucked at it too.

~

Toby waited for Laura to come to bed. After she'd spoken to Bruce, she'd excused herself to her home office and shut the door.

When the guys had left, Toby wandered around the house for a bit, but eventually, he decided to go to bed and watch TV. There were no instructions for how to handle a woman who didn't want help dealing with the issues that she faced.

It was almost ten when Laura walked into the bedroom. She'd let her hair down, and her suit jacket draped over her arm, but she was still dressed in the blouse and skirt she'd worn to work that morning.

Toby watched as she undressed and hung her suit in the closet. She stood in front of the vanity in only her bra and panties brushing her teeth, washing the makeup from her face, and then brushing out her hair.

He knew her routine now, though she hadn't changed into her pajamas. Instead, when she was done, she turned off the lights and walked toward the bed.

She didn't climb into her side, instead, she walked to his side of the bed and discarded the last two articles of clothing. Pulling back the sheets she climbed on the bed and straddled him.

No, he had no idea how to handle women at all. The silent treatment was one thing. The goddess who begged for him to make love to her—he understood that woman. The silent treatment and sex, this confused him more than anything.

Toby placed his hands on Laura's hips and looked up at her.

Her dark eyes studied him, as if she could read his mind.

"I have five appointments next week," she said, but he remained quiet. He knew that opening his mouth only got him in trouble.

Laura lowered to kiss his lips gently and her breasts pressed against his bare skin.

When she sat back up, she pulled her hair over her shoulder. "If they like the house, there will be four weddings taking place here next year, and a bridal shower the first of December."

Toby bit down on his lip and nodded.

Laura rocked back on him and closed her eyes. When she opened them again, they locked on his. "I can either have you invoice me or I can share the profits with you, but I don't want a business partner."

"You're sure?"

"Absolutely sure." She rocked against him again. "I'll take a life partner though."

Toby gripped her hips tighter so she wouldn't rock again. "Is this a proposal?"

Laura shook her head and her hair fell over her face. As she pushed it back, she licked her lips, and rocked against his hold.

"I'm just letting you know."

Finally, he understood something she was telling him.

"That I can handle," he admitted and let his hands wander from her hips to cup her breasts.

"And I want to get married here, too," she said rocking harder against him until he had to flip her onto her back before she caused him physical pain.

"Before my head explodes, let me get a few things straight."

Laura's chest heaved under him and he had to close his eyes to keep his focus.

When he reopened his eyes and looked back down at her, the heat resonated between them.

"Your business is your business. My business is mine."

She nodded and her legs curled around him.

"My house is now a wedding venue."

"Yes," her voice was airy.

He quickly did the math, or as quickly as he could. "So that's six weddings and three bridal showers?"

She blinked hard then smiled, and he knew she realized he'd included hers in there too. "Yes."

"I think we should throw in a baby shower for Kelly too," he offered as he kissed her neck and she moaned beneath him.

"Yes," her voice was nearly inaudible now.

"I think we should move."

Her hands came to his shoulders and her eyes opened wide. "What?"

"Those weddings are only going to spur more business. Just think about it. A Laura Torres Wedding at Maxwell Manor."

She blinked hard again and he could see the shimmer of tears pooling in her eyes.

Toby pressed a kiss to her lips. "I know of a cute rustic house that's available. Maybe we downsize."

CHAPTER 48

Once Laura had taken Toby's offer to use the house, she and her team had gone to work to set it up as it would be used for a wedding or shower. As he'd predicted, all of the weddings had scheduled to use the house. And, just as he'd said, others had wanted to book as well.

Laura knew she and her team had done what they'd set out to do to sell the house to those who were affected by the loss of the other venue, and calling it Maxwell Manor hadn't hurt, but she hadn't committed to the sales of the other wedding dates.

Toby was being a trooper, she thought. He'd allowed strangers into his house to look around, but she only let them tour the house when he wasn't home. There was a great chance he'd feel much different about people in his home when there were hundreds of strangers roaming his property.

Any personal effects and collectibles they had moved down to the guest house when Bruce and Sarah moved into their new house. When Laura had confirmation that someone would be renting her house, she'd hired movers to pack and move her belongings to the guest house as well. They'd managed to lease her house to a corporation who would pay more than the normal renter, but they'd wanted it furnished. As she was hardly home anyway, Laura had decided that her furniture could stay in the house. Anything of value to her was in her office at *Laura Torres Weddings* or she'd already moved it to Toby's.

The last Thursday in October happened to be Bruce's grandmother's birthday and he and Sarah were taking her out to dinner. Since they'd already planned a girls' night, Laura suggested they have it at *her* house so they could plan the shower, and discuss a bachelorette party as well.

Toby thought it would be a good time to have guys' night at the guest house.

Laura opened the door to Catherine and Rachel who had driven up from the guest house together.

"This was the best idea ever," Rachel beamed as she walked toward the front door. "I came with Craig and he took Angela with him when he saw Alex with both of his girls. So I drove up the road with Catherine. Ray had called when we got there and said he was dropping Kelly off here in a few minutes. He was just finding out where all the kids were. Seriously, this is a fantastic night," she continued as she walked into the house.

As Rachel had stated, Ray pulled into the driveway and Kelly eased herself out of the passenger seat and walked slowly from the car.

"Are you doing okay?" Laura asked, noticing that Kelly was showing more now than she had the past few times Laura had seen her.

"Just fine," she groaned. "I have to pee. I always have to pee," she laughed as she walked through the door. "I'll find you guys."

Laura closed the door and watched as Kelly went toward the bathroom, and Laura walked to the kitchen where she heard Rachel and Catherine laughing.

"I read an article the other day about the fire at the Grayson-

Miller Mansion," Catherine said. "It mentioned that they had been completely booked for the season when they burnt down."

Laura nodded as she retrieved the wine from the refrigerator. "They were. Look how much I scrambled, and I only had five events booked there."

"It also said that some of the events were now being held at Maxwell Manor."

That caused Laura to laugh as she filled the glasses she'd set out for each of them. As Kelly walked toward them, Laura pulled the pitcher of iced tea she'd brewed from the refrigerator and poured a glass for Kelly.

"He came up with that on his own," Laura admitted. "Maybe it makes him more comfortable with the situation."

Rachel sipped her wine. "Oh, I've missed this," she said looking at her glass, and then back up at Laura. "Is he okay with it all?"

Laura picked up her glass. "It was all his idea. I want to think he is."

Catherine looked around the kitchen. "I just think of all the things you could do with this house. Let's face it, it's never been homey. And I don't mean that to criticize. I mean this is nicer than any bed and breakfast I've stayed in. And talk about wow factor when you step outside. The back yard alone is worthy of booking events."

Kelly and Rachel agreed, but it still felt wrong to Laura to dream about it, though she had meticulous plans for what she'd do with that house when she got her hands on it. But, that was the Laura that existed before August. Now the Laura who lived within the walls, she just wasn't sure what she would do with the house.

"I have a crew coming the Monday before Thanksgiving to decorate for Christmas," Laura said.

Rachel held up her glass to salute her. "He has one tree. Did he tell you that? An antique aluminum one that he puts in the corner of the game room. And no ornaments. This house decorated at Christmas would be a show stopper."

"Good," Laura sighed. "That's what I want for Sarah." She sipped her wine.

"What do you say we have Thanksgiving here?" Rachel suggested. "One more time while it's just Toby's house, but grandly decorated."

Laura bit down on her bottom lip. "It will always be Toby's house."

"I don't think it will. I think once the weddings happen, he'll want to do something different. And don't think I'm saying because of them. I'm saying this used to be a trophy for him. Now, he doesn't need that. He's going to want something smaller and more geared toward family."

Laura swallowed hard. "He did say he wanted to downsize."

"See? He knows now what this house can net you both. And again, don't think you kicked him out of his own home. He chose to say yes, and he chose to offer it up. As your therapist, I'm telling you to accept that and be grateful."

Laura snorted out a laugh. "My therapist?"

"Everyone needs one, honey," she said, and the other two women nodded in agreement. "But, what do you say to Thanksgiving?"

Laura looked at the other women who nodded in unison. "I think it would be a magical time." She let out a long breath and willed her heart to steady. "Now, let's plan this bridal shower. I have another one we're holding the first week of December, but I want Sarah to be the first bride in this house. Party and wedding."

Rachel reached out and placed her hand over Laura's. "You are very sweet, and that will mean a lot to her."

"I hope so. Because it'll be a trial run for everything," she swallowed hard. "Including my wedding."

The eyes of the three women around her went wide.

"You're engaged?" Kelly choked out the words.

Laura shook her head. "No. But I told him that if we opened the house to weddings, then I wanted to have mine here too. It just seemed right."

The women all held their glasses up to her and toasted.

Okay, Laura thought, maybe for the first time ever, a marriage wouldn't be destined to failure by someone needing something for their personal gain—maybe.

CHAPTER 49

$\mathcal{D}$ress shopping had happened on a Thursday night, and had become a girls' night to remember.

Laura had arranged to have her favorite bridal store stay open late, dinner was catered for the girls and the staff, and hours were spent going through beautiful dresses.

Bruce's grandmother had joined them, as well as Sarah's mother.

With each dress Sarah tried on, her mother sobbed a little harder. "That's the one," she would say. "That's beautiful."

Laura watched Bruce's grandmother as she would nonchalantly wipe away tears. No doubt, knowing that Bruce was loved and well taken care of moved her to tears.

As much as Laura tried to enjoy the gathering with her friends as a social event, it was hard not to be the consummate professional. The sale of the dress to Sarah was still part of her job.

When the right one had been found, it had been obvious by the gasps, cheers, and tears that spread among all of the women.

Laura watched the familiar sight from the doorway, and not from the couches and plush chairs where the others sat. When a hand rested on her arm, she looked to see Bruce's grandmother standing next to her.

"You've given that beautiful girl everything she could ever want for a wedding," she said softly.

"Thank you. That's what I strive for."

"I have to admit, though I've prayed for years that Bruce would find someone and settle down, I'm still a bit surprised it's happening. What I shouldn't be surprised about is the woman he chose. He's loved that girl for as long as I can remember."

Laura's lip trembled. "That's what I've heard."

"And you? I hear you caught the last of them," Bruce's grand-mother smiled up at her. "He was the quiet one," she said. "I prayed for him to find a woman, too, that would love him."

A tear slipped from Laura's eye and she wiped it away. "I do love him."

"I know. I see it in your eyes." She patted Laura's arm. "I look forward to attending your wedding as well."

The guys understood that Toby would be along when he was done with what he needed to do. Laura was at the bridal shop with Sarah and the girls. No doubt that would take hours.

Armed with a bottle of tequila, from the company he'd invested in, a bottle of wine, from the winery in Palisade, and a bouquet of flowers, Toby pulled up in front of the Torres' home and parked.

It was Thursday, and he knew that Laura's grandmother would be there as well. He also knew, even if he wasn't expected, he was welcome.

Toby climbed from his car, walked around to the other side, and opened the passenger door. As he gathered the items from the passenger seat, he heard the screen door squeak as it opened. He turned to see Laura's father standing in the doorway.

In the past few months the man had grown more comfortable around him. Where he would once tuck in his shirt and button it up, now he stood in only his undershirt and jeans.

"Are you missing someone?" he called to Toby.

"Nope. I didn't invite her," Toby said with a chuckle as he closed the car door with his hip and her father let the screen behind him close as he walked down the front steps.

"You came alone?" Mr. Torres asked, his accent thick.

"I did. I would like to talk to you, your wife, and your mother-in-law."

Laura's father nodded. "Juanita is here too."

"All the better." He handed Laura's father the bottle of tequila. "This is for you. It's a company I invested in last year. They're doing very well. I'd like to get your opinion on their product."

Mr. Torres looked the bottle over. "You own this company?"

"A percentage of it."

"This is the good stuff," Mr. Torres confirmed.

"Is it? I'm not much of a tequila drinker myself."

They stood on the front walk for a moment in silence before Mr. Torres looked up at him again. "Have you come to ask for my daughter's hand in marriage?"

There was no way Toby could keep the smile from forming on his lips. "I did, sir. I came to discuss it with all of you."

Laura's father batted his eyes, and Toby wondered if tears were stuck in his throat as well.

That was answered when her father cleared his throat and pushed back his shoulders. "Why do you want to marry my daughter?"

"Because I love her, sir. She makes me feel whole. She brings joy to my life. She…"

Mr. Torres held up his hand and smiled. "I understand. She does the same for me."

"I love her. She's the most magnificent woman I have ever known."

Laura's father ran his hand over his beard. "You've only known her a short time," he said, and laughed when Toby's eyes went wide. "I know things her mother does not."

Toby nodded slowly. "This is true. We've only known each other a few months."

"Would you really have had her arrested?"

Now Toby felt the heat rise in his cheeks. "Well, sir, yes. Yes, if she would have come back again, I would have."

That caused her father to laugh and slap a hand on Toby's shoulder. "That'll be a story to tell the grandkids, huh?"

"I suppose it will," Toby let out a laugh as well, though his stomach knotted.

Mr. Torres broke the seal on the tequila and twisted off the top. He sniffed, then took a hearty swig from the bottle. When he'd swallowed, he blew out a hard breath.

"Yep, that's the good stuff," he said, handing the bottle to Toby. "Take a swig."

That wasn't quite what Toby had wanted to do, but he did as Laura's father asked. Though when he swallowed, he coughed and then blew out a hot breath.

Again, Mr. Torres laughed. "Now you're primed. You can face the firing squad." Again, he slapped Toby's shoulder as they walked into the house. "They're going to rake you over the coals, but they all like you. So just go with it. You'll walk out of here with everyone's blessing."

CHAPTER 50

Sarah's bridal party had been a high tea served in the grand entry of Maxwell Manor. It had been catered, and had been one of *Laura Torres Weddings'* finest.

Laura did her best to be a guest and let Irene run the show, while Amy tended to the wedding that day. But her hand had been in every aspect of planning. She'd also hired a photographer to get pictures of the tea at the manor, so they could use them for promotion, should Laura decide to continue using the house.

When she'd mentioned to Kelly that they would like to throw her a baby shower there too, she'd cried and then begged for a high tea service as well.

A cleaning crew had moved in the moment the tea was over, and decorations had gone up on Monday. Now, the entry was set with tables for Thanksgiving, and Bruce's grandmother ran the kitchen, as she was hell bent on being the one in charge of the turkey.

Laura looked around the room at the people she hadn't known even six months ago.

Kelly helped Charlotte take servings from different bowls and Ray helped Connor use his knife on the turkey Bruce had carved.

The baby was certainly making Kelly a bit uncomfortable, but Laura thought she glowed.

Rachel fed Angela tiny bits of turkey while the toddler tried her hand at mashed potatoes on a spoon. Craig was quick to wipe her face when she missed.

Alex and Catherine's girls sat between them giggling. Catherine did what she could to have Gretchen try the potatoes, and Alex did his best to distract Celia Rose from distracting her sister.

Bruce's grandmother had sat herself right between Sarah and Bruce, which Sarah thought was quite funny. Laura listened as she told stories about Bruce's grandfather and the mischief he and Alex had gotten into as children.

Toby's parents sat at the table with them, and it had surprised Laura when he'd flown them out early to be with them for Thanksgiving. He hadn't discussed it with her, not that he had to, she kept reminding herself. She just hoped she'd made the right impression, since she hadn't been prepared.

He'd also invited her family, including her abuela and auntie. Her mother had, however, made it very clear that they would also be having Thanksgiving at their home with the entire family. Toby had agreed, and to his credit, didn't seem to be put off by the demand.

When the main courses were finished, they began to clear the tables. The noise rose in the house, and Laura thought it sounded like a song. Family.

She thought about the conversation that she and Toby had had early on about weddings that were just about wedding sex, and those that brought families together. Sarah and Bruce's wedding had brought more than their families together, especially for her. It had built her an entire new family she didn't even know she needed.

When she looked out into the entry where the tables were, she noticed her mother, grandmother, and Bruce's grandmother sitting together talking. Yes, even her parents, who came from the tightest knit family Laura had ever known, benefited from this new extended family.

Her attention was diverted when Ray set four bottles of the rosé wine on the counter next to her.

"Do you have enough wine glasses up here, or do I need to bring some up from the bar?" he asked.

Laura laughed. "What's with all the wine?"

"Toby said everyone needed a glass." Ray shrugged.

Laura picked up a bottle. There was nothing new on the label, and it was the wine she'd enjoyed at the winery in Palisade. Was he doing more market research, she wondered as she turned to the cabinet that had the wine glasses.

Ray opened the bottles and poured as Laura counted out glasses. Feeling bad for Kelly, she filled one glass with apple juice.

"He said to pass them around." Ray took the glasses closest to him and handed them to those around him.

When Laura picked up glasses to deliver to her parents and the grandmothers, she noticed they weren't seated in the other room. In fact, as everyone took their wine, they had disappeared.

Ray handed her a serving tray. "Here, put them on here. I'll carry them downstairs."

"Is that where everyone went?"

He nodded. "Toby wants to show off something. Maybe he's plying your family with wine to impress them."

Laura laughed. "I think they're impressed enough. Did you hear my grandmother when she walked into the house?"

"I heard her. I didn't understand what she said, but I heard her."

Ray took the tray and started for the steps. Laura took one more moment to put away the juice and start the dishwasher before she followed everyone downstairs.

She could hear the murmur of voices, but she thought that

everyone would have been talking much louder, especially if Toby was showing off.

When she cleared the stairs, she saw everyone in the corner of the room around an antique aluminum Christmas tree. When had he put up that tree, she wondered and laughed as she saw it.

Toby walked to her, a glass of wine in each hand. "This is for you," he said handing her the wine glass and kissing her cheek.

Laura looked around the room and noticed her grandmother and mother were in chairs by the tree, which had one present under it.

"Toby, what's going on?" she whispered just as Charlotte took Laura's hand.

"C'mon, you have a present to open," Charlotte said as she pulled Laura toward the tree.

When Laura knelt before the tree, she noticed her mother wipe away tears.

"*Mamá*, are you okay?"

Her mother nodded as her father placed his hand on her mother's shoulder.

Laura looked up at Toby. "Open it. Charlotte is here to help. It's killing her," he teased as everyone laughed.

Laura took the box and sat it between her and Charlotte. Together they pulled the bow and ripped off the paper. When she opened the box, she began to cry.

"What is it," Charlotte asked.

Laura pulled out the dress inside. "It's my mother's wedding dress," Laura sobbed. "It's the most beautiful dress I've ever seen. What do you think?"

Charlotte wrinkled her nose. "Yeah, I guess it's pretty," she agreed before Kelly motioned to her daughter to join her.

"*Mamá*, what's this for?"

Her mother batted her eyes and looked toward Toby, who now walked toward them.

"You both told me that you loved her dress," he said. "She told me that you always wanted to wear it—get married in it, and that it sparked your love of weddings. Your auntie told me all about you planning her wedding too."

Laura nodded, her own eyes filled with tears. "Yes. When did she tell you all of this?"

Toby knelt down in front of Laura, who still sat on the floor with the dress in her lap.

"When I went to their house to talk to them."

"You went to their house without me?"

Toby nodded. "Your grandmother gave me tamales," he said lifting his head and winking at her grandmother, who then blew him a kiss.

"Oh, Toby," she sobbed.

Laura watched as he held out his hand to Connor, who then looked up at Ray, and Ray nodded. Connor moved between the people who had crowded around them and handed Laura a black ring box before hurrying away.

Laura's hand came to her mouth. "Oh, God!"

She heard the murmur of laughs.

"Open it," Toby encouraged.

Laura's hands shook as she lifted the top to the box and inside was the biggest diamond she'd ever seen. Again, her hand went to her mouth.

"It's not quite two month's salary," he joked at his own expense, and it was the first time she'd ever heard him refer to his wealth.

"Asshole," Bruce whispered which caused everyone to laugh.

Toby took the box from her and pulled out the ring. "Laura Torres, I have been told that romances are written in tropes. Craig and Rachel, and Kelly and Ray, they have what's called a second chance romance that brought them together. Alex and Catherine, were friends to lovers. Then there is Bruce and Sarah, they were a forbidden love."

Rachel stepped forward. "We had to school him on this. Make sure he watches a Hallmark movie this year."

Laura laughed as she wiped away tears.

Toby grinned. "Then there is you and me. We fall under two categories. Enemies to lovers."

"I don't know that we were ever enemies."

"Friends don't threaten to have the other arrested."

"I suppose you're right."

"And the other is new love," he said. "Well, no matter what romance trope we fall into, all I know is that I love you and I want to spend every minute of my life with you. The good, the bad, the unpleasant, and the unexpected. Laura, will you marry me?"

Her lips trembled as she rose to her knees and wrapped her arms around his neck. "I love you, Toby. I meant it when I said I wanted a life partner."

"You're really bad at this," he teased. "Do I need to write a note and have you mark a box? Laura, will you be my wife?"

Laura laughed as she eased back from him. "*Si.*"

CHAPTER 51

*J*t had been an early Christmas gift, Sarah had said, when she Rachel, Catherine, and Kelly had shown up at Laura's office the Monday after Thanksgiving.

Sarah had taken it upon herself to call Irene, who had seen the rock on Laura's finger and screamed so loud that Amy had run in with 9-1-1 almost completely dialed. With less than six hours of prep time, Laura walked into her bridal shower, hosted by her newest best friends, with her mother, grandmother, aunties, and cousins mixed with her co-workers.

Cake was eaten, stories were shared, and family heirlooms were given in old boxes that had been kept just for her.

Then, Sarah gave Laura her gift.

"I have it under good authority," she said looking at Laura's mother and grandmother, "that Christmas would be a wonderful time to get married."

Laura narrowed her gaze on her family and Sarah. "That's why you're getting married then," she reminded her.

"Day after. Yes," Sarah giggled, "it still counts, but I'm talking on Christmas day."

"Who gets married on Christmas day?" Laura asked, sure that Sarah had lost her mind.

"You. I want you to get married before we do. You should be the very first wedding in Maxwell Manor."

Laura shook her head. "I don't think so. I promised you a perfect, elegant wedding…"

"And that's exactly what I'm going to get," Sarah assured her.

Irene walked around the table and handed her a wedding portfolio. "I know what you would pick," she said. "And there is time to swap out anything you don't like."

Laura opened the portfolio, and inside were the napkins she loved the most, the invitations she's designed years ago, and the colors of pale pink with silver accents.

Laura lifted her hand to her mouth. "You have it all planned?"

Sarah and Irene both shook their heads.

"No," Irene confirmed. "We just gave you a jump start. The wedding planner needs a perfect wedding too. She needs to be the first bride in the house she always dreamed of, and nearly got arrested for." Irene winked.

"And she just happens to have all of the perfect people to make it happen right at her fingertips," Sarah said. "Bruce and I want you to go first. It's very important to us."

"But what about what Toby wants?" Laura asked.

"It's exactly what he wants," Toby's mother said. "I have it on good authority," she repeated Sarah's sentiment from earlier.

Christmas morning, Laura stood in the room which she and Toby had shared, up until a week ago, when he had moved out and to the guest house. He thought it would give them time apart to appreciate what they were *rushing* into, he'd promised with a laugh.

They had decided to live in the guest house until the booked weddings were over. The master bedroom would become the bridal suite that Laura had imagined, and the game room, the groom's suite. All of their furniture would be stored.

Looking in the mirror at herself in her mother's handmade wedding dress, Laura couldn't recall a day she ever thought she looked more beautiful. Slipping into that dress meant everything, she thought. And when *Abuelita* added the strand of pearls to her neck, which she'd worn when she'd married Laura's grandfather, Laura knew that she and Toby were the forever couple—even if it had started out as her needing only one thing from him.

The knock at the door had Laura sucking in a deep breath. But when her father walked through, in a tuxedo, tears stung Laura's eyes and she batted them away as quickly as she could.

"You look very handsome, *Papito.*"

"And you, *mona*, you're all grown up and so beautiful."

Laura moved to him and hugged him tightly. "I was all grown up."

"You'll always be my little monkey," he promised.

This was so much bigger than any multi-million dollar deal, Toby thought as he readjusted his tie for the fourth time in the mirror that had been added to the game room for groomsmen to look at themselves.

When he looked around the space, he thought of the nights he and his friends had shared there. Drinks at the bar. Games of pool at the table. First run movies in his theater. But the more he looked around it, the more he knew it wasn't home anymore, and his gift to Laura was the right one.

Touching his inside pocket, he felt for her gift.

"You look good, man," Bruce placed his hand on Toby's shoulder.

"I can't believe they talked her into getting married before you."

"It's how it should be. Besides, if anything goes wrong today, we can assure our wedding planner will have it fixed by tomorrow," he teased.

When Alex poured them all shots at the bar, Toby and Bruce walked over. Each of them picked up a glass.

"Here's to finding the right girl," Craig said.

"And to sealing the deal before she could get away," Alex added.

"For signing a forever contract, even if you started out rocky," Ray continued.

"To a life full of happiness, my friend," Bruce completed. "No one deserves it more than you."

As they all tipped back their shots, Toby took a moment to appreciate his friends. The guys who happened to have roomed together on the same floor as he had in college. The guys who rounded out the team.

These were his brothers. They had seen one another through happy times and sad times—through deaths and births. These men fought for one another's lives, and each of them loved the woman the others had chosen as their life partners.

Their children would grow up together, and in time, they would all attend the special events and weddings for those children. Together, they would sit in pews and say goodbye to one another's parents, as they'd already done more than once.

"They're ready for you," Rachel stood at the bottom of the stairs in a beautiful dress.

Toby put his glass on the bar. "Let's go."

EPILOGUE

The house had never looked more beautiful, Toby thought, standing in his grand entryway surrounded by lights and trees. It was no wonder Laura laughed when he told her he had one old tree he put in the basement. He'd missed out on years of making his trophy house even more spectacular.

Toby looked out at those who had gathered on Christmas Day to watch him marry Laura. His mother cried, already, and his father's arm gently draped over her shoulders.

Laura's mother sobbed too, but only that morning she had kissed Toby and told him that she was happy Laura had found him.

Laura's grandmother sat in the front row grinning up at him. Perhaps she'd been his good luck charm all along.

Toby's brother nudged him when he saw Laura at the top of the stairs on the arm of her father. At that moment, Toby's knees went weak. There had never been a lovelier sight, he thought.

Her cousin walked down the aisle ahead of Laura, and in front of her, Charlotte dropped rose petals. When she reached the front, Toby knelt and handed her a little box as a gift to his flower girl. Charlotte ran back to her mother to show her the box.

Laura's cousin took her place and the room of relatives and friends stood as Laura and her father walked toward him.

When they reached him, Laura's father kissed her cheek. "Always my *mona*," he said, and Laura batted away tears. Then he turned to Toby and kissed him on the cheek as well. "*Dios los bendiga.*"

Laura took Toby's hand and he moved in to kiss her gently. "You are beautiful."

"Thank you. And you, oh you're so handsome."

"I think the lady who measured me for my tux felt me up," he whispered in her ear and enjoyed the blush that spread across her cheeks.

Laura promised to love Toby for the rest of her life, and he reciprocated. They kissed to cheers from their family and friends, and were announced as husband and wife.

They took their first moments as husband and wife together in the room they had shared which now doubled as the bridal suite.

Toby cupped her face and kissed her deeply. Months later, after they'd kissed at that bed and breakfast, Laura's knees still went weak.

"I love you, Mrs. Maxwell," he said as he trailed kisses down her neck.

"Mr. Maxwell, I love you too, but there is a house full of people we need to greet," she moaned.

"I have to give you your gift."

Laura laughed. "I don't think that's appropriate right this very minute," she said, and he kissed her again.

"No, I have something else for you." Toby lifted the envelope from the inside pocket of his tuxedo jacket and handed it to her.

"What is this?" Laura asked as she opened the envelope.

Laura unfolded the papers she'd pulled from the envelope and read them. Her lips pursed, and Toby noticed the papers move as her hands began to shake.

"What is this?" she looked up at him and her eyes narrowed. It wasn't quite how he wanted her to react.

"It's my gift to you."

"No. No, this is…"

He wrapped his hands around hers, the papers crinkled between them. "It's a gift."

"Toby, this is the deed to your house."

"It's the deed to Maxwell Manor," he grinned when he said the name. "It's the greatest business opportunity you could possibly have, and I want to give you what I can. Imagine being able to exclusively offer weddings here as *Laura Torres Weddings*. You could lease it to others. You could create lasting memories here and offer destination weddings too."

"Oh, Toby, I don't…"

"Take it. Make it great. It's what brought us together."

Laura looked down at the papers. Oh, she could argue with him until they were old, but he'd still want her to take the house she'd dreamed of. And didn't she have all of those plans written out in a notebook already?

"And where will we live?"

He pulled her into his arms and pressed another kiss to her lips. "In the guest house. It's humble. It's just the right size. And it's homey. This," he looked around the room, "was always a trophy. It still is. But our home, it'll be where we can grow as a family."

~

Laura looked down at the ring on her finger that her husband had added, an equally impressive setting as the solitaire, which he surprised her with when he'd slipped it on her finger just over twenty-four hours earlier. Now she stood at the back of the entry and watched Sarah and Bruce exchange vows.

Toby slipped his arm around her waist. "I can't believe your team changed all of this overnight."

"That's what we do," she whispered.

"What's in the bag?"

Laura looked down at the gift bag in her hand. "Catherine gave it to me. I think it's a bag of wishful thinking."

"Why?"

"There's a pregnancy test and a book about what to expect while pregnant. She and Rachel said Catherine just has a gift. Kelly says it's a mediocre gift, but I should try it anyway."

Toby turned Laura to him. "Do they think you're pregnant?"

She shrugged and laughed quietly as Bruce and Sarah kissed and the room cheered.

"It wouldn't be the worst thing in the world, would it?"

Toby pressed a kiss to her lips and as he eased back, he pressed his forehead to hers. "I guess it would be a Christmas miracle."

EPILOGUE TWO

Five Years Later

*C*onnor dribbled the ball from one end of the court to the other with Ray doing his best to block the impending shot from his eleven-year-old son who had already shot up to five-foot-seven.

"Kid, you can't make it," Ray teased, but Connor turned direction, nudged his father, and made the shot Ray said he couldn't. Not to be outdone by her brother, Charlotte took the ball from Connor's hands and shot a layup which warranted a cheer from her mother Kelly who sat on the bleachers with their little sister Christina.

When Catherine and Alex walked into the gym with their daughters Celia Rose and Gretchen, Christina ran across the court to the other girls and they huddled up.

Catherine walked toward the bleachers, travel mug in her hand, and sat down next to Kelly.

"I swear Connor gets taller every week," Catherine said, and Kelly nodded.

"I can't keep up on the clothes," Kelly said wincing.

Both women turned when the girls squealed again, and Rachel and Craig walked through the door with Angela.

Angela carried a bag which she set on the ground and each girl dove into it.

"What did you bring?" Catherine asked as Rachel took her seat next to her.

"We made pom-poms. Now we have a decent cheer squad," Rachel informed them.

"Christina will be in heaven," Kelly said as the next family walked through the door.

Sarah and Bruce walked into the gym, their daughters Mia and Molly holding each of their parents' hands. Immediately the girls' attention was drawn to the other girls who were passing out pom-poms. Sarah knelt down and talked to the girls, hugging her nieces Celia Rose and Gretchen.

Bruce walked across the court giving high-fives to Alex, Ray, Craig, and Connor before sitting down next to Rachel to change his shoes.

"I can't believe your girls will be three next week," Rachel said and Bruce nodded.

"Time flies—finally. I mean, I waited my whole life to finally catch their mother, but now it's really flying."

Rachel laughed. "What did you learn about that Korean preschool?"

"We meet with them next week. Their main goal is to introduce Korean culture to those who were adopted so that they know their heritage, and my grandmother has insisted she pay for it," Bruce said as he kicked off his street shoes and pulled his basketball shoes out of his gym bag. "Sarah's Korean is coming along, but I'm struggling."

"You still want to raise them bilingual?"

He nodded. "Look at Toby and Laura's kids. I think it's an amazing gift to have a heritage and be able to talk multiple languages."

"I think that will be amazing for everyone."

As if Bruce had summoned them, Toby walked into the gym carrying the car seat with their newborn daughter Ashley inside, as Laura corralled their sons Milo and Noah. The family walked toward the bleachers, the boys obviously wanting to see what the girls were doing. Milo at four was a bit shy, but Noah, at two, enjoyed the exploration. However, he would usually wait until Milo was ready to explore with him before taking off.

Toby set the car seat on the floor and Rachel immediately moved to it, unbuckling the newborn and pulling her from the seat.

"I'm sorry, but I need a fix," she said, breathing in the scent of the baby in her arms.

Alex leaned his arm on Craig's shoulder. "Dude, look at her squeezing on that baby. She needs another one."

Craig shook his head. "The two dogs and a girlie daughter are plenty. The fact that the rest of you piled on the kids still baffles me."

Alex shrugged. "Coach would be proud of the regeneration of the team."

The men laughed as they walked toward the bleachers.

Laura sat down and gave each of the boys a toy from the bag she'd carried in, but soon they were off to see what the girls were doing. She laughed, tucking the toys back into the bag.

"It's our turn to host Thursday family night," Laura said, and all heads turned toward her. "We just put in a pizza oven at the manor, so I thought pizza night?"

As was the norm, each family agreed to bring part of the dinner or an activity for the kids.

In time, the basketball game would begin, only Sarah would

often sit on the bleachers with her daughters and Connor would take her place on the court.

And, as had become the tradition in the past few years, at the end of the game the *fabulous five*, their wives, and their children, would gather in the center of the court. Each one of them would put their hands in the center of the circle and on the count of three, they would salute the man that brought them together by shouting his name, "Coach Diaz!"

MEET THE AUTHOR

Bestselling Author Bernadette Marie is known for building families readers want to be part of. Her series The Keller Family has graced bestseller charts since its release in 2011. Since then she has authored and published over fifty books. The married mother of five sons promises romances with a Happily Ever After always... and says she can write it because she lives it.

Obsessed with the art of writing and the business of publishing, chronic entrepreneur Bernadette Marie established her own publishing house, 5 Prince Publishing, in 2011 to bring her own work to market as well as offer an opportunity for fresh voices in fiction to find a home as well.

When not immersed in the writing/publishing world, Bernadette Marie can be found spending time with her family, traveling (mostly to Disney parks), and running multiple businesses. An avid martial artist, Bernadette Marie is a second degree black belt in Tang Soo Do, and loves Tai Chi. She is a retired hockey mom, a lover of a good stout craft beer, and might have an unhealthy addiction to chocolate.

www.ingramcontent.com/pod-product-compliance
Lightning Source LLC
Chambersburg PA
CBHW030405020726
47493CB00003B/954